ILLICIT
DOSE
OF
CHAOS

COPYRIGHT

Edited By: Kimberly See

Front Cover Design By: Diana T. Calcado,
www.triumphbookcovers.com

Formatting By: Wicked Gypsy Designs,
https://wickedgypsydesigns.com

First Printed Edition, 2022

TRIGGER WARNING

"All romances aren't sweet and innocent.
Some are aggressive, possessive, raunchy and raw."
(Regina Ann Faith)

ALSO BY
REGINA ANN FAITH...

The Artistic Series

Artistic Love In The Psych Ward

Artistic Soulmates

The Love Sick Series

Illicit Dose Of Scars

Illicit Dose Of Chaos

ONE

Journee

I start to kiss her as she undresses me. First she takes my shirt off and unhooks my bra. Her hands run freely on my breasts, and I let out a sigh as she squeezes them. Her hands travel down to the waistband of my jeans, unbutton them, and pull them down to my thighs. She looks at me with lust growing in her eyes.

"You are a sight to behold in nothing but your black lace thong." She pulls me close and whispers to me, "Does your boyfriend always like to share you with other women? Because I would love to have you all to myself."

In one swift move, my thong ends up around my thighs, with my jeans. Her hands roam my center, inching closer to my clit.

"Tell me you want me to fuck you. I want to hear it from you," she demands. I'm shocked that this woman wants me to verbalize to her that I want to fuck her.

I stand there, frozen. I have grown accustomed to going numb at this point. Knox has always brought random women—his groupies—to the apartment and watched us fuck each other. Sometimes he would direct us in what he wanted us to do. Sometimes he'd join us. But Knox always fucked me before fucking the other women. It's a vicious cycle I learned to deal with since the first time this happened. I don't want to fuck her. I never want to fuck any of the women Knox brings home, but I have to.

"Fuck me," I tell her in a meek voice.

"What did you say?" she states. "I couldn't hear you."

"Fuck me." I say it louder.

As soon as the words leave my mouth, her fingers are inside me. Her nails are sharp, scratching and scraping at my walls. I can't help but bite my lip until I taste my own blood. I have to muffle a cry, because the pain stings like a bee sting and burns like alcohol on an open wound.

"Shit," I manage to say as she continues finger fucking me.

Meanwhile, Knox is watching this whole thing off to the side. He doesn't say a word. I don't expect him to. He just watches us in amusement, as if we're in a porn video.

I'm up against the bedroom wall as she is finger fucking me. When she finally pulls out of me, there's blood on her fingers. She takes one glance at the blood dripping off her fingertips and throws me on the bed.

"Bitch," she screams.

Knox motions her to come to him as I lie on the bed

in excruciating pain, holding myself. She proceed to kiss him full on the mouth for a good few minutes. Then she holds up her blood-stained fingers. Knox takes them in his mouth and sucks them clean.

"Will there be another time we can meet up?" she asks him.

"I'm not sure. But I have your number. I'll text you," Knox responds.

The woman saunters back to the bed and kisses me again. "Thanks, babe. We'll have to do this again some-time." She leans closer and whispers in my ear, "But next time, it's your turn to pleasure me." She then waves to Knox and leaves our bedroom. Still on the bed, I'm trying to hold back tears. I always seem to every time I'm forced to perform sexual favors for these women. But crying is useless. Knox never gives a shit. He is only interested in the shows I put on with these women he brings home.

"I have to meet Ezra and Reid at the studio. I'll be back later. Take a shower and clean up. You'll feel better after," he says as he kisses me on my forehead, like nothing ever happened.

I don't say anything. I just lie back down and wrap myself in the blankets. I feel sick and don't want to look at him, but I hear him walk out of our room and close the door behind him.

I scream into the pillow, "Fuck. Fuck. Fuck."

Knox is now twenty-six while I'm twenty-two. We've lived together for about four years, since I was eighteen. My dad left for South Carolina a few months after my mother passed away; North Carolina reminded him too much of the good times, when our family was whole. He wanted me to go with him, and begged me on a few occasions, but I had just started booking modeling gigs, and Knox and I had just started dating. When Knox told me I could move in with him, I refused to go with my dad and took Knox up on his offer.

I was so numb at first. Everything Knox and I did together—the sex and drugs—helped me forget about the grief and pain. He would comfort me when I burst out crying for no reason at all. But when Knox got violent, I had no choice but to give in to his demands. I felt trapped. I always gave in. I swore I would never put myself in that position again, yet here I am.

This was all I knew. I was comfortable in North Carolina and didn't want to start a new life, leaving it all behind. So I just take the abuse—and all the fucked up shit Knox forces me to do. I have never told a soul what was happening behind closed doors; not even Willow or Sarai know.

Maybe a shower will do me good. I stumble to our bathroom. I turn on the shower and check the water temperature before I step in. I break down crying as soon as the water hits my body. My tears mix in with the water as I lean against the shower wall. Blood continues to drip down the inside of my thighs as the water rinses away all the guilt and shame.

I'm feeling very anxious when I step out of the shower, so I look in the medicine cabinet to see if there's anything to ease this worry. I look at the many bottles: Tylenol, Advil, and other pain meds. Knox is always stocked up. Playing shows cause all types of aches and pains. Rummaging through the cabinet, I come across a bottle with blue pills in it.

They were for anxiety but clearly marked "Knox."

ILLICIT DOSE OF CHAOS

Since when did he have anxiety? Is it from guilt? Why would he need these?

I take the bottle into our room, contemplating whether or not to take them. But I really need to take my mind off of what just happened.

I open my laptop and start to look for modeling jobs. I search for photography studios in the North Carolina area and come across at least seven different ones. One studio stands out to me, though: Phoenix's Photography Studio. I look through the photo gallery. What really draws me in is all the models are different body shapes, races, and sizes.

Knox's best friend is named Phoenix, and he was their photographer early on in the band's career. *I wonder if this is his studio.* I click on his bio and read through his credentials. He worked with a lot of different types of people, from actors to musicians. I glance through some of the mentioned musicians and clear as day is Supposed Posers. So he is Knox's best friend.

I quickly click on his picture. He looks the same, with his piercing bluish-green eyes and blond hair. He's so handsome. The kind of handsome that would make Knox jealous. *Could I make Knox jealous? Would I want to make Knox jealous?* Hell yes, I would love to. But the thought soon slips away as I dismiss it.

I stare long and hard at the pill bottle, those little blue pills inside. I want to take them and get rid of the shit going on in my head. I open up the bottle and down eight of the pills. I don't care if I wake up or not. I just want to silence the noise in my mind.

I close my laptop and get back into bed. I start getting sleepy. My breathing starts to slow down. The whole room is going in and out of view, so I try to focus on my shallow breathing and the slight convulsions I'm having.

I'm getting scared. I try to see if I can get up, but I can't feel my legs. I'm paralyzed, and now my heart beat's slowing. *What is happening to me?*

TWO

Knox

I'm so fucking ready to head back into the studio, to lay down some new tracks. As a band, we have gotten so successful in these last four years. We were asked to play some festival shows, which is always good. I get to see my other musician friends perform and watch other bands that I admire go do their thing. It's always a fantastic shit show on these festival tours sometimes. There was always some kind of controversy surrounding one or two of the bands playing. The bands in question would be put through hell trying to clear their name, as well as having to fight the media to stop posting outlandish stories about them. But overall, touring is fucking amazing, and I can't wait to get back out on the road.

Once I arrive at the Pavilion, I look for the studio we are in. There are a few other bands practicing tonight. Opium Flames, an alt-metal band who we have had the pleasure of touring with a few times, is also practicing. Tyler, the lead singer, often invited us out for drinks or to local hookah bar to smoke after we finished our sets on tour. The band's guitarist, Kurt, and I felt like kindred spirits, and it was not only because both of our names begun with *K*. We both started playing the guitar in high school, we were both bullied, and we both were the ones to start the bands we are in currently. Kurt and I would often practice different types of riffs and jam out together on our down times when we aren't performing.

"Hey, man. What took you so long to get here?" Ezra says as he comes out of the singing booth as I'm walking into the room.

"Yeah, we started laying down the vocals and drums. We were waiting on you for the guitar," Reid says, kind of annoyed.

"I'm sorry, it's just that . . ." I start to say when Seth cuts me off.

"Well, you are here now, so let's not dwell on this too much and get to work," he states.

So I grab my guitar, head into the booth, and record my part of the song that we're working on. Seth calls us all over after I'm done to discuss an important matter.

"As you all know, someone tried to hack into Knox's computer to gather personal information about him," Seth explains.

"Why? Does someone have a personal vendetta on you?" Ezra says, concerned, as he turns to face me.

"Not that I am an aware of. I've already changed my passwords, so I should be okay now," I state.

"No worries. I will be adding extra security at your shows," Seth states. "In fact, I'm already on it."

"Do you think that's necessary?" Reid questions. "Knox said he already changed his passwords."

"I don't know what information this guy gathered on Knox before he changed his passwords, so it's better to be safe than sorry," Seth states. "I know that this is a hard pill to swallow, but we have to try and keep Knox safe."

"Yes, of course. How are you dealing with all of this, Knox?" Ezra asks.

"I'm dealing with it the best I know how. I've been taking anxiety meds because of it too," I tell them honestly.

"Shit. It's affecting you that much, Knox?" Reid asks.

"I can't sleep at night sometimes, knowing that this guy could be at any one of our shows and do god knows what to Journee and me."

"Trust me. Nothing will happen to you or Journee. Rest assured, we will catch this guy," Seth states.

Seth goes through all the security measures and precautions that will be taken at each show. After we hear more about the steps in keeping Journee and I safe, we feel more at ease with this whole situation.

We spend two more hours in the studio, laying vocals, drums, and guitar down for three more tracks, before calling it a night.

"Hey, are you guys up to get some drinks tonight?" Reid asks as we're packing up to leave.

"Not me. I have a long day tomorrow," Seth replies.

"I'm down," I state enthusiastically.

"Me too," Ezra concurs.

"Hey, do you want me to see if the guys from Opium Flames would like to join us?" I ask them. "They're down the hall from us."

"Sure. Would be great to catch up with them," Ezra says.

"Have a great time," Seth says as he's heading out the studio door.

I leave to see if Opium Flames is almost finished practicing. I knock on their studio door and wait.

"Hey, Knox. It's good to see you. What's up?" Tyler, the lead singer, asks, leaning on the door.

"Are you guys done with practice? The guys and I are headed to Drinks on Me, if you want to join us."

"Hell yeah, we'd love to. You know we aren't the type to pass on drinks!" Tyler states. "We'll meet you there, okay?"

When we all arrive at Drinks on Me, we're surprised at how packed it is. I immediately ask Mickey, the manager, to put us in a private room. None of us want to be hounded by fans tonight. We just want to chill.

"Come with me, guys. I'll take you around back." Mickey quickly steers us outside, around to the private room in the back. He tells us he will personally take care of us. We can order anything we want off the menu and he will pay the tab.

"Thanks, Mick," I say.

"You know I love to take care of my regulars."

I ask the guys what they want to order beside the drinks, and the consensus is some kind of appetizer. They don't care what. They just want something to eat.

I turn toward Mickey. "We'll have boneless wings, potato wedges, and mozzarella sticks."

"Coming right up, guys." He leaves the room in a hurry.

"Thanks for inviting us out with you guys," Tyler states. "We've been working hard on our new album, and we definitely needed this."

"No problem. You know we're always down for hanging with you guys," I say.

"So what's the new album going to sound like?" Reid asks.

"It still will be a signature alt-metal sound, although we are playing around with different drum progressions, guitar riffs, and vocals," Kurt answers.

"I'll have to sit in when you lay down the tracks. I would love to hear the new riffs," I tell Kurt excitedly.

"You guys will have to. Maybe we could even do a special collaboration, like a bonus track," Jared, the drummer of the band, adds.

"So are you guys working on a new album?" Tyler asks us.

"We're working on a few tracks here and there, in hopes to make a new album soon."

"Will there be a new sound to your music?" Jared asks.

"Like you guys, we try to change our sound up just a tad to keep the listeners on their toes," Reid says.

Mickey returns with our appetizers and beers. We thank him before he leaves, and continue talking about us making albums and other things music related.

I check the time on my phone and notice I have a voicemail. It's from Journee. I must have missed it while we were rehearsing.

Journee: *Knox, please come home soon . . . I don't know what's . . .*

That's odd. She knew I was at the studio and would be home when I was finished. This was two hours ago, and she hasn't tried calling me since then. I'm getting worried. So I quickly call her back, but get no answer.

"Hey, guys. I'm sorry but I have to go," I tell the guys frantically.

"Are you okay?" Tyler asks, concerned.

"It's my girlfriend."

"Journee? What's wrong with her?" Ezra asks.

"She called me and left a voicemail. But I just tried calling her just now and got nothing."

"That's so unlike her."

"I know. I'm going home to see if everything's okay."

"All right, man. Call us if anything," Reid says.

I rush to my car and speed the whole way to my apartment. Thankfully, I didn't drink that much—maybe one or two beers. I don't need to be pulled over by the police, especially not now. I just need to get home—fast. At first my thoughts are racing and I can't think straight. But as closer I get, everything slows down. It seems like time stopped. As soon as I reach my apartment, I sprint to the front door. I survey the place, and it doesn't look like anyone broke in. It's actually pretty tidy. Journee doesn't like a messy apartment. She always makes sure it's present-able for people who might visit us. But Journee isn't in the living room, and there's no sign of her being in the kitchen either. *I was probably panicking for no reason, she's most likely sleep in our bed.*

So I casually walk into our bedroom. My racing heart calms down when I see her lying on our bed. I had nothing to worry about. I wonder what her earlier voicemail was about, then. I go over to kiss her, and she's so fucking cold. I try to shake her awake, but she doesn't stir. I'm los-ing my fucking mind at this point. My nearly calmed heart back up and is beating manically out of my chest. *Why won't she wake? What the fuck happened?* That's when I look over and see the bottle of my anxiety meds on the floor. Pills were spilling out of it. Holy fuck . . . she over-dosed. I rush to call 911.

"I need someone quick," I say frantically to the dispatcher on the phone. "My girlfriend overdosed."

"Is she still breathing?"

"She's cold," I manage to say.

"Where is your location? Someone will be there right away."

I give the dispatcher the address to my apartment and tell them to hurry. I'm freaking out. *What the hell, Journee? This is so unlike her. To overdose on pills?* I stay in our room and watch over her until the ambulance arrives.

THREE

Journee

I wake up in what seems to be a hospital room. While most hospital rooms have white walls and smell sterile, this room's walls are powder blue, and I can smell flowers. A wooden cabinet stands to my left. It's wide open, revealing extra blankets, gowns, gloves, etc. The room itself is very modern looking. Even the blanket that's covering me isn't your typical hospital blanket. It's covered in pink flowers and is wrapped securely around me, but I am still shivering. I can't remember what happened. It was all a blur, but I blacked out. I don't even know how I got here.

"Fuck, Journee, you scared the shit out of me," a voice says as I focus hard on trying to figure out who's talking to me.

There sits a guy in front of me. But my mind is playing tricks on me. I go to open my mouth to ask him who he is, but nothing comes out. So I bite my lip, look at him with a blank stare. I shake my head back and forth, growing frustrated with the lack of ability to properly form my words. These pills really did a number on me. I blink twice to try and see who it is.

"Journee, it's me. Knox," the voice says after a little while.

"Knox?" I'm still a little disoriented.

"Yes, babe, it's me. How are you feeling?" he says.

"I'm okay," I say. "What happened?,"

"You overdosed on my anxiety pills. The doctor injected you with something to wake you up."

I gasp as I remember. Knox—he is the cause of this. I start to shiver again. I've taken a variety of different kinds of pills in order to deal with my mom's passing. But what Knox doesn't know is that I also take them to numb the feeling I have when he forces me to have sex with his random groupies. I was fucked up in the head because of him.

Suddenly, there is a knock on the door, and the doctor comes in. "Journee Watson. You are one lucky young lady. We were able to get everything out of your system."

"Thank you, Dr. Langley," Knox says. "I really appreciate all you did to help her."

Dr. Langley looks at me.

"Is it okay if I ask your friend to step out of the room for a second?"

I look at Knox. He seems to be trying to play it cool about this whole situation, but I can tell he's distraught.

"I'll go get something to eat," Knox finally says.

"I won't be long. I just want to speak to Miss Watson about some things."

Knox nods and leaves my room, closing the door behind him.

"Miss Watson, I shouldn't have to tell you that you ingested a very high, very dangerous dose of medication," Dr. Langley states. I nod, and he gives me a small smile. "But that's not the only thing I want to talk to you about."

"Oh? What else do you want to speak to me about?" I say, concerned.

Dr. Langley takes a deep breath. "Journee, we saw bruises on your body as we were examining you."

Fuck, I didn't realize they had to examine me. I lean my head back on the pillow, trying to figure out what I'm going to tell him. I stare blankly at Dr. Langley for what seems like eternity.

"Has your boyfriend ever laid his hands on you?" he questions.

"No." I try to say it with confidence. I don't want him asking me any more questions.

"Do you know the cause of these bruises?"

"Lack of various vitamins," I tell him. "I'm trying to incorporate more vitamins into my diet. I have to because I'm a model."

Dr. Langley looks at me and gives me another half-smile. *Can he tell that I am bullshitting him?* I'm not a good liar. I despise having to lie to Dr. Langley, but I can't tell him the truth and risk getting Knox in trouble. It's fucked up that I'm covering for his ass after all he has put me through over the years. But it is what it is.

"I will prescribe for you to get vitamins B12, C, and K as soon as you are discharged," he says.

I give him another nod as someone knocks on the door.

"Come in," Dr. Langley states

Knox comes in with a bag of chips and sits in the chair. The doctor glances at him, then back at me.

"I'll leave you two alone. You should be good to go home around noon."

Knox sits there, eating his chips silently until the doctor leaves. "Do you want some of my chips?" Knox asks me.

"No," I say, annoyed.

"What's wrong? Isn't it good that Dr. Langley said you can leave soon?"

"Do you know what he asked me about when you left?"

"I haven't got a clue," he says.

"They examined me and saw bruises on my body, Knox. I had to lie to Dr. Langley to cover your ass."

"Oh? I never left bruises on your body."

"That's a fucking lie," I say angrily.

"Okay . . . Okay . . . Babe, I'm sorry. I was scared shitless that I might have lost you, and I wouldn't have been able to deal with that."

"You always say sorry, but shit never changes, Knox."

"This time, I promise. This was the wake-up call I needed," he says apologetically.

I lie back on my pillow, close my eyes, and drift back off to sleep.

"Jour. Jour," Knox says as he lightly shakes me. "It's time to go."

"I have to get dressed first," I say as I get up slowly and walk over to the window sill, where my clothes are laying. I grab them and stumble to the bathroom to throw them on.

"Ready?" Knox says when I come out.

"Yeah, let's get out of here."

I gather the rest of my belongings. Knox and I walk hand in hand up to the front desk to have them discharge me. When we get to the front desk, the receptionist looks between Knox and me, shaking her head. She asks my name, types something in the computer, then prints out some paperwork.

"Sign here at the *x*, and then initial here," the receptionist states.

I grab a pen from the cup on the desk to sign and initial.

"Here you go," I say, handing her back the paperwork.

"Thank you. Enjoy the rest of your day, Miss. Watson," she says.

The receptionist gives us a quizzical look as Knox and I turn to leave.

"What the hell was up with her?" Knox whispers as he holds tightly to my hand.

I shrug my shoulders. "I don't know. Maybe she is jealous."

We get in Knox's car and head back to our apartment. *Was this actually a wake-up call for Knox? Will he finally change his ways?* I replay the conversation in my mind as he's driving us home. I really want to believe that my attempted overdose was enough for him to think twice about the way he treats me, but part of me feels like it's all smoke and mirrors.

Like it's just Knox talking to himself, knowing there isn't an ounce of truth in his words. Maybe I should have told Dr. Langley the truth. Then Knox would have no choice but to be forced to get help. But I don't want to deal with the endless questioning I will have to go through. I don't want to relive those memories, relive any of the abuse. I'm such a fucking coward, but I can't. It's too traumatizing.

We step inside the house, and I walk to our bedroom because I need a shower and want to lie down. But Knox grabs my hand before I walk away.

"Babe, I can't tell you how lucky I am to have you in my life. Yes, I know I fuck up sometimes, but I love you and will always love you," Knox says, seemingly remorseful. "I would love to make you something to eat. What would you like?"

I just stare at him, not knowing if I can trust his words. I really want to, but something inside of me just won't let go of what he put me through. The last thing I want to do is mention what's happening to me to my father. I know my dad will probably kill Knox, as well as be pissed at me for not telling him. So just enduring the abuse Knox inflicts on me seems like the easier option.

I give Knox a wry smile, before saying "Chicken and Broccoli Alfredo sounds absolutely delicious right now."

"Anything for my girl." He kisses my forehead.

"I'm going to go freshen up and lie down," I tell him.

"Go ahead. Just relax. I'll bring the food to you."

Knox goes into the kitchen to start cooking, while I go into our bedroom to take a shower. It was one hell of a couple of days. I need to collect my thoughts and relax my mind. I need to figure out my next moves regarding my modeling career. I need to get more serious in trying to find a more stable gig. These random shoots I've found online and booked were good when I first started out. But I definitely need something more consistent.

I throw my yoga pants on with a Supposed Posers hoodie and climb into bed to watch TV until Knox is finished cooking. I flip through the channels, and I find a reality show. I started watching reality shows to escape my reality. It's became my guilty pleasure because I realized some of these girls lives are just as fucked up as mine is. I had finished two episodes of *Seeking Love* when Knox comes strolling in the room with a tray that has a plate of chicken-and-broccoli Alfredo , garlic bread, and a glass of white wine.

"Thanks, babe smells so good," I say as he sits the tray in front of me.

"It taste as good as it smells," he states.

"You ate already?"

"No, not yet. I'm going to get my plate. But I did taste test it before I brought it to you."

"Oh, okay. I will wait for you, then, to eat," I say.

"You start eating. I want to hear what you think," he says, heading back to the kitchen.

Knox is right. It's delicious. He's certainly gotten better with his cooking skills. Maybe better than me now, or at least comparable.

Knox returns with his tray of food. He sits the tray on the dresser and starts to undress. I watch him, trying to suppress the memories of him torturing me on different occasions. I don't know what is worse—the sex he makes me have with various women or when he fucks me himself.

I definitely think it's the latter, since I never see the women I have sex with ever again. But I see Knox every single day. I push down the memories, continue to eat, and focus on the TV.

After Knox changes into his lounge clothes, he grabs the tray and comes to bed. I turn the TV down a smidge.

"So what are your plans for tomorrow?" I ask.

"We have an impromptu gig, and meet and greet," Knox says.

"Oh . . ."

"You don't have to go, Journee. I rather you not. You need to recuperate."

"I know. Dr. Langley said I should give myself a few days to a week."

"See? Doctor's orders." Knox smiles as he twirls the pasta around his fork and puts it in his mouth.

As soon as we both finish eating, Knox goes to put our plates and trays back into the kitchen. Then we continue watching *Seeking Love* until we drift to sleep.

FOUR

Knox

The guys and I are in a van heading to the outdoor venue. The venue sits fifty to one hundred people. It also has a lawn area located in the back to sit roughly twenty-five to fifty more people. It's a medium-sized stage with a cover overhead held up by steel beams on each side. The other band that was supposed to play had to cancel last minute, so Seth asked us if we wanted to take their place, and it was a unanimous *yes*. We are all stoked to play some newer songs for the crowd. This will give us a feel for which songs our listeners resonate with more, which songs we should add on the upcoming album.

Seth's driving the van while Ezra, Reid, and I are discussing our set for the show. We decide to play three newer songs and two older songs.

"I meant to ask you about Journee. Was everything okay with her?" Ezra says, concerned.

"You rushed out in a panic last night, so we were just wondering," Reid adds.

I don't know how to tell them that Journee almost overdosed on anxiety meds—let alone my anxiety meds. I know if I told them the truth, hundreds of questions would follow, and I don't feel like addressing any of them. The two they just asked are already more than I'm comfortable with. If it were up to me, I would have dodged all questions about last night.

"She's fine," I lie. "Just a little stomach bug. Nothing too serious."

"Oh. Okay. I hope you don't catch it," Ezra says.

"Nah . . . I'll be fine. Don't worry."

"Are you all set with your song list?" Seth says.

"Yes, all good to go," Ezra responds.

"Ready to rock this show," I add.

As soon as we reach the venue, we unload our equipment with the help of the staff. Then we chill backstage until it is our turn to perform. It is a beautiful day for an outdoor concert. The sun's shining, but it isn't too hot. The crowd is large and a lot of people are wearing their band shirts. A few are even wearing our shirts, even though we are a last-minute addition. The concert promoters must have announced the change.

Ezra and Reid decide to hang with some of the other bands that are performing, while I just want to lay low until we were on. I grab a sub sandwich, water, and chips from the massive food spread the event staff set up for the bands. As I'm finishing up my food, Ezra and Reid scroll in and grab some for themselves.

"All the other bands want to go out to a hookah bar after the show," Ezra states.

"Well, are you going to go?" I ask.

"Reid and I of course want to go, but we know with Journee being sick, you may not feel up to it."

"Yeah, umm . . . maybe some other time," I state somberly.

Speaking of Journee, I should check up on her before we take the stage. She was alright when I left this morning, though I know she felt a little guilty not being able to come today. I told her that getting better is her number one priority right now and that we would have other concerts in the future. She's been to a lot of our concerts already. So while Ezra and Reid discuss their plans later tonight, I text Journee to see what she was up to.

Hey, babe, how are you doing? We're here at the venue, waiting to go on.

Journee: *I'm doing fine. I just ate the leftovers from last night. Now I'm watching TV. After this show, I'm going to take a nap. So sorry I can't be there.*

It's okay. We'll have other shows. You've been to a majority of them anyway.

Journee: *I know . . . It's just that I love watching you guys perform. But okay, I'll let you go. I love you.*

I love you too.

I know I told her to stay home and rest, but I'm going to miss seeing her face in the crowd. When she's better and can come to our shows again, I'll play for her and only her. Nothing else will matter in that moment. She'll have all my attention. But I don't want to make her feel even more guilty than she already does, so I just let it be.

Ezra, Reid, and I watch the other bands from the sides. Each band brings something different. Two of the bands have a slight reggae vibe going on. The other band is nu-metal. They are okay . . . if you're the type of person who doesn't mind screaming through the whole song. I personally am not a fan, but the band does have an interesting sound.

After the third band, it is our turn to take the stage. Before we even stepped out, we hear the crowd shouting out our names. This is music to my ears. Being added last minute to the roster sometimes it's a bad thing, with audiences all set to hear the originally scheduled band. So to hear the enthusiasm of the crowd waiting for us is an adrenaline rush.

We play two new songs first, like we agreed to. Both "The Answer" and "Guess Again" are very well received by the crowd, which makes us excited to record the rest of the songs we came up with. We're working so fucking hard to perfect them before we take them to the studio.

We are ushered backstage again after our performance. While waiting for the meet and greet with the fans, I text Journee. She was so bummed about missing us play brand new songs live, but I let her know that she'll be the first one to hear the other songs we are working on for the album. That cheers her up tremendously, and I'm glad.

We are told there are only a handful of people who bought passes, so the meet and greet is only supposed to last half an hour. Thank God. It has been a long day, and I am ready to go home to Journee.

They have set up a long table, maybe eight feet long, with the right number of seats for each band and their members. There is also merchandise, courtesy of the different band managers. It is cool to see to way each of the table was decorated. Ezra, Reid, and I sat down at the table assigned to us. We are very grateful to be able to sign autographs and meet our fans up close and personal. It always takes me back to the time I met Journee four years ago, at one of our own meet and greets. Meeting her and going on those first few dates was the best time of my life.

The crowd is ushered out of the venue after the meet and greet is finished. The event staff are breaking down the tables and packing up the merch to give back to each of the band managers. The band members themselves are all either standing around and talking to each other, on their cell phones, or with their girlfriends.

"Man, we should have invited Willow and Sarai," Ezra says, looking at one of the other guys talking with his girlfriend.

"We should have, but would that have been fair to Journee?" Reid says.

"You could have invited them," I tell them. "I know Journee wasn't able to come, but you deserve time with your girls, even when mine's not here."

We all eventually migrate toward each other and talk details for the hookah bar.

"You sure you don't want to come?" Reid asks me.

"Nah. But I'm sure it would be enjoyable." I smirked, knowing they'd have a good time.

In the distance, I see this really pretty girl. She is standing way in the back, where the lawn area is located.

She is hanging with a few of her friends. I wonder why she didn't come to the meet and greet. Maybe she didn't have passes, but I sure as hell would have made an exception for her. She has long black hair, and, from what I can see, she is wearing a long multicolored gypsy skirt with a powder-blue tube top. One of the perks of dating a model is that Journee's fashion sense has rubbed off on me. So much that I have developed a knack for   describing what people are wearing.

"Hey, we are getting ready to head to the hookah bar now," Ezra says, breaking my concentration on the girl.

"Oh . . . all right. I'll be heading back to my apartment soon. I'll catch a ride back with Seth," I say.

Ezra and Reid leave with the other bands. I am still standing in the same spot after they leave. *I should text Seth to see where he was or if he left thinking I was going to the hookah bar with the rest of the bands.* To my surprise, the girl I was admiring is still hanging around with her friends. Maybe I won't have to get a ride from Seth. This girl might live close enough to drop me at my apartment. Who am I kidding? I'm trying to get laid by this girl.

I stroll over to where they are. Her friends point me out and whisper something in her ear before they leave.

"Hey," I say casually.

"Hey. How are you doing?" she asks.

"I'm good. Where did your friends go?"

"They had to leave. They carpooled, and some of them had to get back home."

I know she is lying. They definitely weren't whispering about carpooling. They probably left so she could talk to me alone. Then they are gonna tell her to spill the details later.

"My name is Knox," I say. "And yours?"

"Chesca."

"So, Chesca, were you and your friends at the concert?"

"Yes, we saw you guys perform. You were amazing," she gushes.

"Why, thank you."

I want to tell her that I'm amazing in the bedroom as well. But you know, first impressions. Chesca seems like she was fiery and fierce. I could tell by the way she was dressed. That skirt she has on makes me want to slide it off her body. Maybe she is a belly dancer. Either way, I certainly want to see her moves. By looking at her, Chesca comes across as the type of woman who doesn't take any shit from guys but can get down and dirty in between the sheets. There is only one way to find out, and tonight may be the night I get the honor of experiencing that side of her.

"Do you want to get out of here?" she asks.

"Yeah. What do you have in mind?"

"We could go to my place. Chill out and watch a movie . . . If you're up for it," Chesca says coyly.

Oh, hell yes. I was so up for it. Friends with benefits? I have had no problem being a fuck buddy with the female friends I had in the past. Since those girls ended up being a one-or two-week sex fest, I was willing to take this chance with Chesca for even one night.

"That sounds perfect."

I quickly shoot Journee a text, telling her I am out with the other bands and not to wait up for me. I need something she can't give me right now. Fucking up is what I do best, and I've been doing that a lot recently, so why stop now? I will make it up to Journee one of these days, but tonight isn't one of them.

I climb into the passenger seat of Chesca's black Subaru Legacy. She turns on her Bluetooth audio, which is connected to her phone. The music starts to play, and I realize it is one of our songs.

When "The Muse" starts to play through the speakers, Chesca turns slightly to me without taking her eyes of the road and flashes me a smile. Yup, this girl knows what she's doing. She wants to get laid as much as I do. I'm not mad at her at all. This is strictly for the benefit of both of us. One night, no strings attached.

When we arrive at her condo, she parks her car in her driveway, and we both get out.

"Lead the way," I say, motioning my hand like a magician getting ready to perform their first trick.

Chesca looks at me and then motions me to follow her. When she opens her front door, she tells me to have a seat on her couch.

"You have a nice living room," I state as I looked around. "You decorated it yourself?"

"Yes," she says with a light chuckle, "with the help of Pinterest. Do you want to do some tequila shots?"

"Umm . . ."

I am hesitant at first because doing a round of tequila shots will most likely get us fucked up, and I am not too sure if that is a good idea.

"What are you leery about? You aren't leaving anytime soon. You'll have enough time to sober up," she explains.

"I guess you're right. Let's do this," I say with enthusiasm.

Chesca goes into the kitchen. She comes back with a tray of four shots, two shots for each for us.

"Thanks." I pick up one of the shots and down it. Chesca follows suit with her first shot.

"So you liked the show?" I say after the burning sensation subsides in my throat.

"I did. You are a very talented guitarist. When did you start your band?" Chesca asks curiously.

"When I was eighteen. I didn't want to go to college, and music was my passion, playing the guitar in particular. So one day I made an ad looking for a drummer and a singer. I posted it on all my social media platforms and eventually got an email from both Reid and Ezra. As they say, the rest is history. And here we are." I eye another one of my shots before asking her, "What about you? What do you do for a living?"

"I'm a model. I started when I was eighteen. I was in shows and pageants growing up. I loved the thrill of dressing up and being someone else for that one moment in time. So you can say I was always meant to model, ever since I was young," she explains.

Chesca took her last shot of tequila. Just watching her down the last shot is such a

turn on for me, and we haven't even kissed yet. I finally

down my last shot of tequila and am feeling a slight buzz. I look over at Chesca who has a mischievous grin plastered on her face. I think to myself I wouldn't mind showing her a few things.

"What are you thinking about?" Chesca say, breaking me out of my thoughts.

"You really want to know?"

"Yes."

"I'm thinking about how badly I want to kiss you right now."

"Oh . . . so why don't you? I don't bite." Chesca gives me a seductive wink.

After Chesca gives me her permission, I go in for the kiss. I start off slow at first. Then I slip my tongue into her mouth, and she lets out a soft moan. My hands go straight to her breasts. I rubbed them through her powder-blue tube top. Chesca starts to kiss me more aggressively, and soon I find myself lying with my back against the couch. Then something snaps, and it isn't me this time. Chesca starts to trail her hands to my belt buckle and begins undoing it.

"What are you doing? What about the movie?" I ask her, though I really don't want her to stop.

"Fuck the movie." She smirks and continues to loosen my buckle. "I'm ready to suck you off."

Chesca motions me to sit up, and removes my shirt. She pushes me back down and begins to kiss my neck down to my chest and splatters kisses over my stomach. As she moves closer to my cock, I can feel myself getting hot and bothered.

"Shit, I'm going to come." I give her a stern warning.

"Good. I'm ready for you." She puts my cock to her lips and pushes it to the back of her throat.

I can't wait any longer and spill my load into her mouth. Even after she swallows it, Chesca continues to suck on my cock. She sucks on my cock like it is the first and last thing she will suck on for years.

Chesca gets off me and wipes her mouth with the back of her hand. She then proceeds to flaunt her ass back to her fridge. She grabs a bottle of water and chugs it down. Damn, this girl is feisty.

Chesca saunters back. "So was that as good for you as it was for me?"

"Hell yeah," I state, still on my high.

"Well, why stop now, playboy?" she whispers in my ear. I look at her, ready and willing for whatever else she has in mind. "You want to take this to my bedroom?" she asks.

Just then Chesca kisses me full force on my mouth, biting my bottom lip. We go into her room and continue what we started. And holy hell—it is more than I expect. Chesca blows my fucking mind . . . and everything else there is to blow.

FIVE

Journee

K nox texted me last night, telling me that he was going to a hookah bar with the other bands, so I was home alone for the whole night. I didn't mind it much, but I did miss him a little.

I take it slow in the morning. I am still recovering from my stint in the hospital, and I don't want to push my luck. I fix some waffles and have a glass of almond milk for breakfast. Then I text Knox to see when he will be home. It takes him a few minutes to respond, but he says he had stayed over at Ezra's apartment since Ezra lived close to bar.

I figure I will be alone for a while, so I decide to give Phoenix's studio a call. I have nothing to lose and everything to gain. I go back to our room after I clean the kitchen. I grab my cell from the nightstand, and the number I jotted down on a piece of paper. I take a deep breath before dialing the number. It rings a couple times before I hear a women's voice answer.

"This is Phoenix's Photography Studio. How may I help you?" she asks.

"I'm a model looking for work. Are you looking to hire any new models?" I ask confidently.

"Yes, we are always looking for new models. Can I have your name?"

"My name is Journee Watson," I tell her.

There is a few minutes of silence and rustling of paper.

"Can I ask you a few questions?"

"Sure."

"First, how old are you?"

"I'm twenty-two."

"Can you describe yourself?"

I'm five-eight, light skinned, hazel eyes, curly red hair, and freckles. And I weigh 115."

"That's sound perfect," she says as I hear muffled voices on the other end of the phone. "I have one more question to ask you. Do you have any headshots?"

"Yes, I have a few head shots."

"Okay, great. Let's see . . . Phoenix has an available slot at two p.m.? Does that work for you?"

"Yes, it does."

"Fantastic, Journee. I'll pencil you in for that time.

See you at two."

I wait till we get off the phone to silently scream. Hell yes! I can't believe I might have an opportunity to model for Phoenix. I really need this job. I search my closet for something to wear. I want to impress the hell out of him. First impressions are everything, after all. I decide on a black suit with silver earrings, a silver necklace, and sparkly silver high heels. Then I jump in the shower and wash my hair. I want it to be super curly, so I add Cantu when I get out. I feel hella confident as I get dressed. I am going to kill this meeting. Phoenix won't know what hit him when I walk into the room.

I plug into my GPS the address I found on the studio's website and end up arriving early, so I sit in my car for a while. It feels good to not be bothered for once. I mean, I love Knox—he's a genuinely a great guy—but he's very touchy feely . . . Actually, what do I expect? He's a guy. Sometimes, I don't mind. Other times I want a break, but he doesn't get that.

When it is almost meeting time, I get out of my car and walk up to the cream-colored building. It has several floors, at least four or five. I enter through the doors and see a board with the companies' names and floors on it. I scan the board for Phoenix's name. Fourth floor, room four-two-seven. I take a few deep breaths in the elevator to calm my nerves. I really want to get signed. I step out of the elevator and try to figure out where to go. To the right.

I walk past three offices before I reach Phoenix's studio. I enter through the glass door and approach the desk. There is a girl about my age at the desk. She has long black hair and green eyes, and she is wearing a black short-sleeve polo shirt with "Phoenix" embroidered in the upper right corner.

"Hello, I'm Francesca, but most people call me Chesca. How may I help you?" she says.

"My name is Journee. I have an appointment with Phoenix," I tell her.

"Oh, the red-headed chick . . . Oh . . . I'm sorry, how unprofessional of me," she apologizes. "Have a seat. He should be out in a few minutes.

I just smile. Phoenix really needs to hire more professional people.

I decide to flip through a random magazine as I wait for Phoenix. I look up when I feel someone standing in front of me.

"Journee Watson. Journee? I knew your name sounded familiar," he says with a smile.

Holy Shit. Act cool. Don't blow it. He is handsome—even more handsome than the picture on his website. He has bleach-blond hair, but his dark roots are clearly starting to grow out. His eyes are a bluish-green color, and he has a fitted graphic T-shirt on, along with black jeans and black sneakers.

I smile back. "So we meet again."

"How's Knox, by the way? Does he know you are here?" Phoenix questions.

I don't want to tell him that I'm here on my own accord. That Knox doesn't know I have an appointment with him for a possible permanent modeling gig. So I reply, "Knox is fine," and leave it at that.

"I see you met Chesca. She's just filling in. She's actually one of my models. Let's step into my office," he finally says.

She's a model, not a receptionist. That explains it. I feel better now.

His office is small. He has pictures of his models on the wall. They are diverse in shape, size, skin tone, just like on his website. That means I don't have to watch my weight as strictly as I am.

"So you described yourself to my receptionist. She wrote everything down and gave it to me to look over. I want to ask how long have you been modeling."

"On and off since I was eighteen," I respond.

"Okay, that's good. Did you bring your headshots?"

I reach into my bag and pull out three different headshots. He looks at them very intently.

"These are amazing. The camera really loves you." He leans over his desk. "Now I have to ask you the tough questions."

"Ummm . . . okay."

He laughs. "Don't worry. Journee, I'm kidding. These questions are just protocol. I want to get an idea of what you are comfortable doing and not doing. Bathing suits, lingerie, nude?"

"Everything except for nude," I tell him.

"Okay, fair enough. I just want to let you know I will respect your decisions, and I will never pressure you to do something you don't want to. I have a contract for you to sign that explains the terms and details. Are you okay so far?

"Yes." I am getting anxious. "Does . . . does that mean I got the job?"

"Journee, you had the job as soon as I looked over your stats. Plus, now that I know who you are, I'm definitely signing you on."

"Thank you, Phoenix. I really appreciate this opportunity."

"No problem. Is there anything else you would like to discuss before you sign the contract?"

I shake my head. "No"

"All right, if you have no more questions, here's the contract." He hands me a small packet. "I need you to read it over and sign."

I skim over everything. I trust Phoenix and know he won't lie to me. So I ask him for a pen and sign my name.

"Welcome aboard," Phoenix says as he takes the contract back.

"Thank you," I say, smiling.

"I would like you to be here around nine tomorrow morning."

"No problem. I'll be here," I say with a shy smile.

Then he dismisses me with a lingering smile of his own. "Have a great afternoon, Journee."

Chesca stops me on my way out of the studio. "Hey, Journee. How did it go? Did you get signed?"

"He told me to come back tomorrow at nine am," I tell her.

"Oh, for the bathing suit and lingerie shoot?"

"That's what's happening tomorrow morning?"

"Yep. I'll be doing the shoot with you," she says excitedly.

"Oh, okay. I'm looking forward to it. See you in the morning."

I leave the studio feeling proud. I finally landed a stable modeling gig. Knox will certainly be excited for me. I can't wait to tell him once I get back to the apartment. But I don't think I want him thinking about his best friend taking pictures of his girlfriend.

When I enter the apartment, Knox is on the couch, watching a game. He immediately turns down the volume and focuses his attention on me. "Babe, where were you? I thought you would be home when I got here."

"I had a meeting with a photographer," I tell him in excitement while keeping things vague. "I'm a signed model now."

Knox's eyes light up and a smile stretches across his face as he gets up to hug and kiss me. "Congratulations. I knew all that hard work would pay off. Fuck yes, my baby is on her way to super model status!"

"I wouldn't say super model status just yet, but I'm certainly going in the right direction."

"Hell yeah, you are. Who did you sign with?" he questions.

"Connor Abrams," I lie. "I've worked with him in the past."

"Oh. He's awesome. The band never worked with him, but he was someone Seth was considering before he went with Phoenix. He wanted to give a newcomer a shot. And I'm glad he was willing to do that. Phoenix was and always will be a kick-ass photographer," Knox explains.

"Yeah . . . So how was the concert?" I ask before he can dig any deeper.

"The concert was fucking amazing. The crowd loved the new songs we played."

"That's awesome. How was the hookah bar afterward?"

Knox shifts on the couch, like he is hiding something. I don't know what. Then again, I am hiding the fact I signed with Phoenix, so I guess we are even.

"It was fun. Always a riot when the bands get together after the show," he finally says.

"So what's on the agenda for tomorrow?"

"We have to meet with Seth to go over the logistics of our next music video. Also gotta find another model for the video," he explains.

"Oh, okay . . . I have my first photoshoot in the morning."

"My baby doing her thing. I'm so proud of you. You sure you don't want to change your mind and be in the music video?"

"No. I want to focus on print ads. But I'm sure you'll be able to find someone easily."

He pouts. "I know that. But she wouldn't be you."

"Aww . . . babe. You're making me reconsider."

"Really?" Knox responds to me, questioning if I really meant what I said.

I chuckle. "Just kidding."

"Damn it, Journee."

"Trust me. It'll work out fine."

"What do you want me to tell Sarai and Willow when they see you're not there?"

"Just tell them I was signed with a photographer and will be too busy," I explain. "But I'm going to call it a night for now."

"I'm going to finish watching this game. I'll be in there after."

"Good night." I give him a lingering kiss before heading to our bedroom.

The next morning, I wake up excited for my first photoshoot with Phoenix. Knox is still asleep, so I am careful not to wake him. I quickly jump in the shower to wash my hair and shave. I throw on my black yoga pants and a white crop top when I get out.

"You look sexy as hell," Knox say as he sits up in the bed.

"Oh, I didn't want to wake you. I'm sorry."

"Don't be. I have to be getting up soon anyway to meet with Seth," he explains. "Kick ass at today's shoot."

"Thanks. I definitely will."

I kiss Knox goodbye, but he pulls me into him.

"Shit. Please. Knox, not now," I plead. "I have to

go."

"Oh, you're no fun." He lets me go with a pout.

I make a quick smoothie in the kitchen and yell to Knox that I am leaving.

I go to the studio around eight-thirty. I park my car in a space and sit there, reflecting on how far I've come in my modeling journey. Here I am, getting ready to do my first real photoshoot as a signed model. It is so unreal and surreal at the same time.

"Morning, Phoenix . . . Morning, Chesca," I say, entering the studio.

Phoenix and Chesca are looking through some magazines. I guess they are both getting inspiration for the shoot that is going to take place.

"How are you doing today, Journee?" Phoenix asks, addressing me. "Are you ready? We'll be shooting the bathing suit and lingerie ad this morning. That room"—he points to a room off to the side—"has everything you need. Go pick out what you want to wear."

"Come on, Journee," Chesca says, pulling me along. "This is the fun part."

There are racks of bathing suits and lingerie inside. Plenty of options to choose from.

"This is better than shopping because another thing is that whatever we wear, Phoenix lets us keep," Chesca tells me with a wide grin.

"That's so cool," I say, looking through the bathing suits and lingerie.

We each choose a bathing suit and a lingerie set

for the both of us. I try them on in the bathroom, and I feel beautiful. The ones I picked, they fit like a glove. I look in the mirror, and saw a girl who is partially broken because of her boyfriend, but growing stronger with each passing day. The first shoot is for a bathing suit ad, so I step out of the bathroom with what I need on.

Phoenix shows me some poses that he wants. I have to laugh. He looks so funny trying to show me how he wants me.

"I'm glad I amuse you," Phoenix says when he sees me laughing.

This feels different than when I am with Knox. I am so used to lying to myself and everyone else about what I feel inside. But Phoenix isn't demanding. Thanks to him, I feel at ease the whole shoot.

The entire shoot takes a few hours. Afterward, Phoenix sits Chesca and I down to discuss some exciting news that he can't wait to tell us.

"Chesca, I have a director who is looking for an extra model to be in a band's music video. Would you be interested?" Phoenix asks her. "I can call him to let him know I have an interested model," he adds.

"Hell yes! I would be extremely interested. Call him, Phoenix!" Chesca says, grinning widely.

"Great. I'll call him right away," Phoenix urgently says before turning to me. "Journee, I wasn't sure if you would be interested in an opportunity like this."

"No, it's okay. I'm just focusing on print ads for

right now," I tell him.

"Good to know. Now I know what to look out for if we get requests from other studios. Changing the focus back to photography, he said "Journee, all I can say is, wow these pictures are going to be amazing."

"I look forward to seeing which ones you choose," I tell him.

When we are done for the day, I tell Phoenix how grateful I am he chose me as one of his models and that I can't wait to see what other shoots he recommends me for.

Chesca stops me on my way out. She hosts girls nights every now and then. She wants my number to invite me, so we exchanged numbers.

SIX

Knox

After Journee heads out, I get up and get ready, throwing on my skater jeans and black converse. I also wear a graphic tee with lyrics from "Sacrifice," and my leather jacket to top it all off. The meeting at the Pavilion doesn't start until ten. I have plenty of time, so I take a moment to just look over our bedroom. A lot has changed over the years.

Journee and I recently did a much needed make-over. It was time. We got rid of the mosaic painting that was hanging above our bed. We replaced it with a blinged-out *J* and *K* letters, with black roses woven between them. Her old model photos and my old band pictures were taken down and replaced with new ones. We even added a few pictures of us together. We didn't have any before. The comforter, which was once black and silver, was swapped with one a deep blood-red color. I really love the upgrade. It is very edgy, just like

Journee and I.

I go into the kitchen to fix myself breakfast. I scarf down a packet of strawberry Pop-Tarts and chug a glass of almond milk. Then I fix my hair in the bathroom real quick before I head out. I just spike it up on top and flatten the sides with gel. I really want to keep the top and shave the sides down. Maybe one of these days.

I texted Seth I am on my way to the Pavilion. He texts back that he, Ezra, and Reid will be waiting out in the lobby. I see them as soon as I walk through the building's sliding glass doors. They are waiting on a cushioned bench behind a rounded wooden table. It kind of reminds me of a snail shell.

"Hey, guys," I say, grabbing their attention.

"Hey, we're just looking at some models for the music video," Ezra states.

"Oh . . . Where did you find these models?" I ask.

"Phoenix has a photography studio. Dorian called him to see if he had any models we could hire," Seth explains.

"Oh, wow," I say, sarcasm dripping from my mouth. "Phoenix is a fucking big shot now."

"Apparently," Reid states.

"Why are we looking for another model? Isn't Journee supposed to be in the video?" Ezra questions.

"Journee wants to focus on print ads," I explain.

"And she's okay with some other model being in the video?" Reid says inquisitively.

"Yes. She is," I state.

"As long as she's okay with it," Ezra responds.

I watch over Seth's shoulders as he scrolls through different headshots. "These models are so beautiful. How about her," I say, motioning Seth to stop scrolling.

"She's cute," Ezra says.

"I agree. But you should be the one to choose, Knox. We have Willow and Sarai," Reid states.

I look closely at the picture and read her name that is on the bottom of the head shot.

Oh shit. It *is* Chesca, the girl I fucked the night I told Journee I went to the hookah bar. How awkward, but how ironic. I definitely want her to be in the video now that I know who she is.

"I would like her to be in the video."

"Are you sure?" Seth asks.

"I'm positive."

"All right then, I'll tell Dorian to call Phoenix after we're finished here and book her."

With that squared away, we move on to discussing the concept for the music video to "The Answer." Dorian, the director had the idea to pose a question at the beginning of the music video and have clues throughout the video until the answer is revealed at the end.

"That's a dope ass idea," I say.

"I thought so too," Seth agrees. "How about you guys?"

Ezra and Reid agree.

"When are we shooting?" I ask Seth.

"Two weeks from now," he responds. "I reserved a studio for a few hours if you guys feel like laying down some rough demos of the new songs you've been working on."

I don't have anywhere to be. Journee is still at her photoshoot, and I don't know how long it will be. I have plenty of time. So it is up to the guys.

"Of course. Let's do this," Ezra states.

"We can demo some of the songs we didn't have a chance to get to last time," Reid suggests.

We follow Seth to the space he booked. "I'll watch you guys a little for the first half," he says. "Then I'll step out to call Dorian.

We warm up a bit before going over lyrics. As soon as Ezra steps into the booth, it is like the song is a knife, and he lets his heart and soul bleed out. He has a voice like no other. The sincerity, passion, and angst— he belts out each word. It makes me remember why I asked him to be our lead singer.

Reid then steps into the drum booth and hits the drums like he is mad at the world. He says that his idol on the drums is Travis Barker. Reid knows that he can never drum the way Travis does, but he could try and come close. Travis inspired Reid to want to start playing the drums. So I think Reid is channeling his inner Travis Barker on the tracks we decided we are going to demo.

After Reid finishes, it is my turn to record the guitar part. In this particular song, there is a guitar solo, so I am given permission to "free" play the riff. I already have the notes in my head and written down. I know the gist of how I want to play it. But when I finally execute it, the riff comes out more kick-ass than I had hoped. We definitely have another hit on our hands and can't wait to record the full track.

We record one more track before wrapping it up. Seth comes back to catch the tail end of us working on the last song demo.

"You guys are fire," he says. "I talked to Dorian. He called Phoenix to let him know we wanted to book Chesca."

I am starting to have mixed feelings about seeing Chesca again. I mean, it was only a one-time thing, but still. I don't want the guys to find out I slept with her. But they really can't talk; I know their secrets. And they wouldn't want me to "accidentally" slip up and air their dirty laundry.

Two weeks flew by like that and I am driving back to the Pavilion to shoot the video. I can't wait to see how this video will turn out, since the concept is so fucking cool. I am immediately taken to wardrobe when I arrive, but I have yet to see Chesca. I am little nervous about that. Turns out she and the other two are getting their hair and makeup done in another room.

"Are Willow and Sarai excited to be in another video?" I ask Ezra and Reid as I am going through the outfits our style team picked out for us to wear.

"Yeah, they are so excited. But they did question where Journee was and why she wasn't going to be in the video," Ezra explains.

"What did you tell them?" I say nervously.

"We told them right before Checsa arrived that Journee wants to focus on print ads, just like you mentioned," Ezra states.

"How did they take it when you told them that?"

"That were a little bummed at first because, you know, they got closer to Journee and became friends. So to have another model take her place is weird. But they'll get over it," Ezra says.

Dorian peeks his head in. "We are starting in five minutes." We quickly finish up and head out.

"Hi, I'm Francesca. But I go by Chesca. It's nice to meet you. I'm grateful for this opportunity," Chesca says as she extends her hand.

She is drop dead gorgeous. Her outfit hugs her curves in all the right places. It makes me think about that night. I can feel myself hardening as I think about wanting a repeat performance. The odd thing is she is acting like we'd never met before. Maybe she wants to play it cool. We were both slightly buzzed that night, so maybe . . . Either way, she isn't budging, so I play along.

I shake her hand, trying to push the thoughts of wanting to fuck her again out of my mind. Professional, Knox. Be professional. "Thanks for coming on board. I appreciate it."

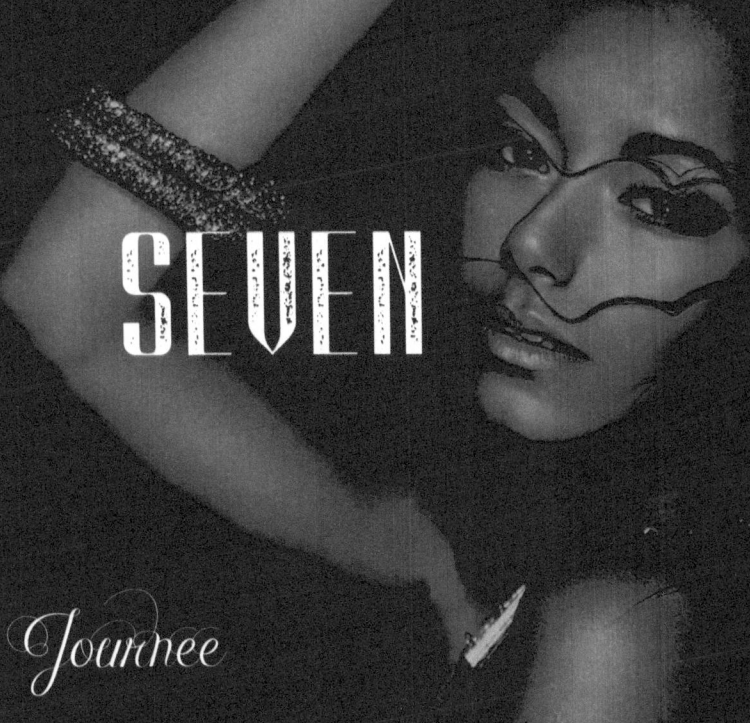

SEVEN

Journee

Knox has his music video shoot today. I have mixed feelings about not being in the video. I do want to focus on print ads—that isn't a lie. But I can't help but think of what he might have told Ezra and Reid. Do they think we broke up, and that is the reason I am not going to be in the video?

What about Sarai and Willow? I wonder what Knox will tell them? They are the first real girl friends I have met through being with Knox. Even though I really can't worry about it, it's bothering me a little.

I have a personal goal of trying to make a name for myself. I am only known as being Knox's girlfriend. That's another reason why I want to focus on print ads. People see me as his model girlfriend where as I want to stand on my own two feet. I want an established career for myself.

Plus, I wonder who the new model they hired is. Is

she prettier than me? Comparable to me? I can't help but feel a hint of jealously. Will she be in all of their videos, now that I won't be? Will she become friends with Sarai and Willow? Will Sarai and Willow forget about me? All these thoughts consume my mind.

Phoenix texted me last night and asked me about doing a solo shoot. It will be my first solo shoot in a while. He explained this brilliant idea that had been ruminating in his mind for a few weeks. He thought I would be the perfect model for it.

I arrive at his studio at nine-thirty. Phoenix immediately takes me into his office to go over the shoot. "I see you in a formfitting formal dress."

"Oh?" I sit across from him, an eyebrow raised. I already love the idea.

"Yes. I'll take a few photos of you in a few formal dresses. You'll be standing in front of a green screen, which I can use to create a background behind you. It's a simple shoot, but I know you'll be breathtakingly gorgeous."

Phoenix shows me the room where he keeps all the formal wear. There is a sea of colorful dresses to choose from, and he tells me that I am free to choose any dress I want. He doesn't care.

I pick out three different dresses, then change into the first one. It is a sparkly silver mermaid-style dress. I absolutely love it. It hugs my curves, and my ass is to die for in it. Phoenix is going to be floored.

"Oh my God." Phoenix gasps when I walk into the room. You look like a fucking princess. I love it."

"Thank you."

"Hey, save it for the camera."

Since this is an impromptu shoot, Phoenix lets me pose how I want. He takes dozens of photos before we wrap up. He is mulling over the photos when I come back from changing into my street clothes.

Phoenix is good. He can make a can of paint look like gold. I understand why Knox's manager hired him as the band photographer back when they were starting out. But I watch his expression as he stares intently at the photos. It is that of adoration—adoration for me.

"Hey, Journee, I didn't see you walk back in. Do you want a glimpse of the photos I took," Phoenix asks.

"Of course I want to see."

He is holding his camera, so I stand behind him and glance over his shoulder. He brings the camera up to my eye level and starts to scroll through each picture. I lean into him to get a closer look. We are so close, I can smell his cologne. It is elegant and sophisticated. It smells like an expensive night in New York City.

"Stop. I love that one," I tell him excitedly.

"This one," he responds, going back to the previous photo.

It is the photo he took of me in the sparkly silver mermaid-style dress. The backdrop is white hanging lights that illuminate and make the dress pop. I look like angel.

"Yes, that's absolutely magical," I gush.

"You think so?" He gives me a sly smile. "I love this one too."

Phoenix's smile takes my breath away. Everything

about him is perfect. I think I am slowly falling for him. I know nothing can happen between us. But I wonder if Knox wasn't my boyfriend, could we be together?

He suddenly pulls away slightly. "Umm . . . it will take me a week or two to touch these up."

"That's fine. I look forward to seeing the finished photos."

"Journee, are you hungry?" Phoenix sounds hesitant.

"Starving."

"I made some roasted chicken, potatoes and asparagus last night for dinner, and I have plenty of left overs," he states.

"Oh that sounds so delicious."

"I don't normally invite my models to my condo. But you aren't just any model."

I mean, we do know each other. It's not like I'm a stranger to him, but I think about what might happen if I were to go to his condo. He knows Knox is my boyfriend, and they're best friends. I don't think he would try anything.

"Okay," I finally say.

The gated community he lives in is quite posh. All the lawns we pass are neatly trimmed. Some have the sprinklers going.

"Welcome to my humble abode," Phoenix says when we arrive. He urges me to go inside first.

I smile. "Thank you."

He tells me to take a seat on his couch while he warms up the food. "What would you like to drink? I have juice, water, or wine?" he yells to me from the kitchen.

I think about it. I drink wine on occasion, but given the circumstances, I don't know if wine would be an intelligent choice right now. There is obviously chemistry between Phoenix and me. But when we first met, truth be told, I thought Phoenix was a creep. I couldn't stand the way he glanced at me while I was around Knox. Having feelings for someone I once loathed is hilarious to me. I don't want to let my defenses down. So water it is.

Phoenix comes into the living room and puts two bottles of water on the glass coffee table, winking at me. "I'll be right back."

I take a swig of water and start to play with the top of the bottle after putting the cap back on. I guess I get that from my dad. I can't help but wonder what is going through Phoenix's mind.

He returns with two plates. "I hope you like it. I'm not the best cook, but I try."

"I'm sure it's scrumptious. It smells so good," I say as I broke a piece of chicken with my fork.

"So?"

"What kind of chicken is this? It's so yummy."

"Lemon pepper. I'm so glad you like it. It's just me here, so I don't get a lot of feedback on my cooking skills," Phoenix says with a chuckle.

"Oh? I'm surprised you don't have women falling at your feet."

"Well, no one is as lucky as Knox," he says shyly

.Would you like any more?" he asks after a while.

"No, I'm good. It was very tasty. Thank you for inviting me over."

He puts our dishes away, but when he comes back, he stands as if on pins and needles, thinking of what to say.

I break the silence between us. "Well I think I should get ready to go?"

I stand up and head to the door when Phoenix stops me by gently grabbing my arm.

"Wait, don't go," he pleads.

I turn to face him, my breathing unsteady. I want to kiss him so badly, to feel his lips on mine, but I don't know why. I look into his eyes, hoping he will get the hint.

"God, you are so beautiful," Phoenix says as he leans in to kiss me.

He starts off slow, then deepens the kiss. I immediately kiss him back. He leads me to the couch and lays me down, my back hitting the pillows. He continues to kiss me, his mouth moving from my mouth down to my neck. Then he unbuttons my top and continues trailing kisses down. Both of us are breathing heavily, like we need each other for air. Phoenix gets up off me after a while and motions me to stand in front of him. He pulls my jeans and panties down, and admires me for a few moments. Then he sits me back down on the couch.

"Spread your legs open," Phoenix gently commands. His eyes linger on my body as his hand brushes against my cheek. So I do exactly what he desires of me. With my legs spread, Phoenix gets on his knees and begins eating me out. I throw my head back and dig my nails into the pillows on either side of me. Phoenix grips my thighs to steady me as I start to grind against his face.

"Holy fuck." I scream in pleasure.

Phoenix flicks his tongue over and around my pussy. At one point he inserts two fingers inside me. Phoenix hits me in that one spot that causes my eyes to water.

"I'm not done with you," he says seductively in my ear after taking his fingers out.

He picks me up and carries me to his bedroom. The sheets on his bed are soft, unlike Knox's. I watched Phoenix take off his jeans and boxer briefs. He isn't as huge as Knox is, but he is well-endowed none the less.

He undresses me himself before crawling on top of me. "Are you sure you want to do this?"

"Yes," I respond. "More than anything,"

We aren't just about to have sex. He is about to make love to me, treating me gently as if I were still a virgin waiting to be deflowered. Phoenix takes his time as he entered me. He doesn't want to do anything to hurt me. It feels so fucking good. I get so lost in him, I forget how painful sex can be. I forget about the scars around my heart.

We lie next to each other after. Phoenix feels different. Unlike Knox, who is hot and cold at the same time, Phoenix feels like a safe place to retreat to. He feels like home.

He wraps his arms around me, pulling me into his chest. His heart is beating rapidly. "Can I ask you something, Journee?"

"Yes, sure. Anything."

"How did he hurt you?"

"What?" I say, puzzled. I look away from him.

Phoenix turns my face to face him again. He lifts my chin to meet his gaze. "Journee, how did he hurt you?"

"Umm . . ." I break eye contact.

This will be the first time I tell someone what Knox has done to me. For four years I lived with these "incidents," haunting me. They aren't affecting me as much while I am on shoots, but am I ready to come clean to someone? Especially if that someone is Knox's best friend?

Tears start to fall from my eyes as I gaze into his. They are filled with hurt and concern . . . for me.

"He . . . he . . . forced me to do things I didn't want to do. He was always forcing me," I stammer through my words.

He pulls me back into his embrace. "Shit . . . Baby, I'm so sorry," Phoenix whispers.

I was so emotionless for the longest time after it happened. Yes, I would cry to myself, but no one knew the full extent of my pain. So confessing to Phoenix feels like the first step to really acknowledging what Knox has done to me.

"I didn't realize that he was the one doing this to you," he says, sounding a little frazzled, but continues. "You know, I would snap photos of you at various events when you were with Knox. I thought you were gorgeous, and I wanted to find out the secret you hid behind your eyes."

"My secret?"

"I could see that you were hiding something. I thought maybe Knox was behind it. But I didn't want to think that of my best friend."

"Why didn't you say something to him if you thought that?" I question.

"I didn't want to get in the middle of it. I liked you for a long time, Journee. I just didn't want to ruin the friendship Knox and I had," Phoenix explains. "I could sense he was jealous of me. If I would had called him out on it, he would have most likely denied it. He would have thought I was trying to steal you away from him."

"Maybe that would have been better," I confess. "If you had stolen me from him."

Phoenix stares at the ceiling for a long while trying to gather his thoughts. *Is he feeling guilty? Guilty he didn't call Knox out, that he didn't save me?*

EIGHT

Knox

I try texting Journee several times to let her know I am on my way home. She doesn't respond, which is strange.

I go straight to bed when I get home. It was a long-ass day and I am exhausted. In the middle of the night, I feel Journee's breath on my neck. I don't know when she got in, but I am grateful she did and that she is okay. I was getting worried.

Journee and I haven't had a chance to have a day to ourselves in a while, both of us busy with our careers lately. In one of the texts I sent Journee last night, I asked her if we can spent the day together. I figured we can visit my parents. It has been a while since we visited them too. It's not like we don't want to. We are just busy, like I said. My parents already practically consider Journee their daughter-in-law. They even promised to look after her, with her dad in South Carolina.

I asked my mom what they were doing this weekend, if she would like visitors—namely her son and his
girlfriend. She messaged back immediately, said she and
Dad were going to have a chill weekend, so she was more
than happy to include us in their plans. It took an hour to
drive to their house, sometimes two depending on traffic,
so Journee and I would likely have to leave in the afternoon
or early evening. The plan was set. I just have to convince
Journee. I was hoping to talk about this with her last night,
when I sent her a text, but I guess I have to wait until she
wakes up to ask her.

I get up and freshen myself up a little before I make
breakfast for us. Just something simple, not too elaborate.
I hear Journee's footsteps enter the kitchen just as I am
finishing up.

She is wearing her pink silk robe and her fuzzy
white socks with pink hearts on them. Journee's red hair is
underneath a bonnet that matches her socks. She still looks
a little tired. Maybe she had a long day yesterday too.

"Morning, babe. I made omelets," I say.

"Thank you." Journee sits down at the table. "It
smells delicious."

I quickly fix both of us a plate and hand one to
Journee. "So I was wondering if you'd want to spend
the weekend with her parents. We haven't seen them in a
while."

She keeps her eyes down, focused on her omelet.
She seems distracted by something.

"Journee?"

"Oh . . . Oh, yes, that would be fine. I would love to
visit your parents for the weekend," she says.

"Great, because I just let my mom know that we were coming and she was so excited."

"Okay." She sounds hesitant.

"Is something wrong?"

Journee puts her fork down and glances at me. She looks like she is struggling with something. She isn't her normal self. Maybe something happened last night. I thought this weekend trip would be good for us before, but now I am sure it was what we needed.

"I'm just thinking about something. It's no big deal," she finally says.

"Do you want to talk about it?"

"No . . . I'm fine, really." She continues eating her omelet.

"I told my mom we'd head out either this afternoon or evening. Is that okay? It will give us enough time to pack and get ready before we hit the road."

"Yeah, that's fine," Journee says as she rises from the table. She gathers her plate and puts it in the dishwater. Something is really off with her, but I am not going to push it. If she wanted to talk about it, she would have.

Instead she says, "I'm going to get dressed and start packing."

"Come here for a second," I say gently.

Journee walks over, and I wrap my arms around her. She is stiff at first but then slowly relaxes into my embrace.

"Babe, I don't know what's wrong, but I want to make it right," I state.

She pulls away and immediately casts her eyes to the ground. I lift her chin so our eyes meet. I can see that they are glassy like she is about to cry.

"Please talk to me," I beg.

"There's nothing to talk about," she says in a flat, monotone voice. "I'm going to go pack now."

And with that, Journee leaves me standing in the kitchen. I hope this isn't an indication of what the weekend at my parents will be like. I tell myself that I will give Journee some space to clear her head, so I clean up the kitchen before I start packing myself.

Journee eventually comes out of our room with her duffel bag in her hand. She places it by the door and sits down on the couch to watch TV. I watch her flip through the channels until she settles on something before I go to our room.

I pack three pairs of jeans, five different types of shirts, a handful of socks, some sleepwear, hair gel, cologne, and other toiletries. I throw everything in my bag.

Afterward, I take my duffel and put it by the door, next to Journee's. I go into the kitchen and throw a few snacks in a Ziploc bag for the road. Then I join Journee on the couch. She is in the middle of watching a reality show. I don't know what her fascination with reality shows are, but the shows she watches are very entertaining, to say the least. When the show is over, I ask Journee if she is ready to hit the road. I text my mom to let her know we are on our way.

The drive to my parents' house takes exactly an hour. There is hardly any traffic, thank God. The tension between Journee and me eases away during the drive. We talk about how both things are going with our jobs: I talk about our recent music video, while she talks about the last shoot she did. I do notice, however, she is a little nervous talking about it. It is like she is skating around certain details, which is weird in a way. But at least we are talking again.

I park my car beside the curb, next to the driveway. I grab our bags from the trunk before Journee and I walk up the driveway to my parents' front door. I ring the doorbell twice and wait.

I smile at Journee, and she smiles back. It is a smile worth cherishing. Whenever she smiles at me, it turns me into mush. I love her so much that it hurts. I don't know what I did to deserve her, but I'm thankful. I have fucked up many times, causing her pain, but it's because I'm afraid to lose her. I'm scared to lose her, honestly. I'm a sadist, and it's just who I am. I don't mean to cause Journee pain, but I always make it up to her in one way or another.

The door opens, and my mom appears in the entryway. Rose Foster isn't a typical mom. She is my hero. I wasn't an easy child to deal with growing up. Especially after I got kicked out of high school and had to be homeschooled for the entire three and a half years. She sacrificed a lot for me, and I'm thankful for her. Not many mothers would put up with a trouble child like I was.

My mom embraces me and then embraces Journee. "Journee, how have you been?"

"I've been good, Rose."

"Let's go inside. You guys must be hungry after that hour drive. There's lasagna, garlic bread, and salad."

Journee and I follow my mom inside. We set our bags by the steps before we go into the kitchen. We sit at the table while my mom makes us each a plate.

I get out of my seat. "I can help."

"Don't be silly. You are our guests. Your job this weekend is to relax and enjoy our company," she says.

"You sure?"

"I'm sure. Now sit back and relax."

"Where's Dad?"

"He is outside by the pool," she says.

"I'll be back. I'm going to let him know Journee and I are here."

I make my way outside to the pool. My dad is sitting at the patio table, reading a book.

"What are you reading?" I ask him.

"Knox. I'm so glad you're here." He gets up from his seat and hugs me.

"Me too. It's been a while," I say, hugging him back.

"Is Journee here too?"

"She's inside with mom."

"You better be treating her right," he warns.

"I am," I tell him.

I want to head back toward the house, but not before saying, "Mom made lasagna, if you want to join us?"

"I'll be in there in a minute."

I leave Dad out by the patio and go back inside. Mom and Journee are engrossed in some type of conversation.

"What's with all the laughter?" I say with my eyebrow raised.

"Just sharing some of your childhood memories with Journee," Mom states.

"You were quite the character," Journee says.

"I still am. You love me for it right, babe," I say jokingly.

"You know I do."

I give Journee a kiss on the forehead. She responds by endearingly squeezing my hand.   "Is your dad going to join us for dinner?" Mom asked.

"He said he'll be in, in a few," I tell her.

I sit at the table next to Journee, who is already eating. My mom hands me a plate of lasagna, and I join Journee.

"Mom, I love your lasagna," I say. "It's my favorite meal you cook."

"I know. That's why I fixed it," she gushes while preparing her and dad's plates.

"Thanks, Mom. You are the best."

That's when my dad comes in. My mom puts his plate in front of him as they both sat at the table.

"Dad, have you checked to see if there is any information on the guy who seemed to be stalking me?" I ask.

"I've tried to find out more information on this guy, but he seems very smart. We can't trace anything on this guy. But we'll keep trying," he says reassuringly.

"Am I in danger, Knox?" Journee asks, concerned.

"You have nothing to worry about, Journee," I tell her.

"Well, I hope they catch this guy, whoever he is," my mom interjects.

"Me too," I respond.

We finish eating dinner. Then Mom shows Journee and me to the guest room.

"Do you mind if I take a shower, Rose?" Journee asks my mom.

"Of course, darling. Right this way."

Journee grabs clothes to change into and follows my mom to the bathroom. I hear the shower turn on after a while.

Mom then comes back to the guest room. "I brought some graham crackers, chocolate, and marshmallows for s'mores . . . if you are up for dessert." Your father is setting up the fire-pit in the back."

"Yeah, we would be up for that. Just give us a minute. We'll be out there."

"You know your father and I are so glad you both decided to come."

"We're glad to be here too," I say and kiss her cheek.

"Well, when you guys are finished, meet us out back." She skims her hand through the top of my hair and then leaves.

I quickly change into gray sweats and a gray hoodie, hoping Journee will get turned on. Maybe I'll get lucky later tonight. It has been a minute. I knew after her overdose, she didn't feel up to it. Cue in the moment I fucked up because of that fact. But again, I won't make excuses. It's in my nature to fuck up.

"Hey, handsome," Journee says as she enters back into the guest room.

She wearing her black yoga pants and her white long-sleeved crop top. She looks sexy as fuck. If it weren't for us making s'mores tonight with my parents, Journee and I would be locked in this guest room.

"My parents want to make s'mores for dessert," I tell her.

"Yum, s'mores. I haven't had s'mores in a long time."

"I want dessert . . . But not that kind of dessert." I wink at her.

"Calm down. You'll get what's coming to you," she says coyly. "Be patient."

There is a knock on our door. "You and Journee almost ready?" she says with a light laugh. "Everything is set up and ready to be roasted."

"Yeah, Mom. We're coming," I say, giving Journee a seductive look.

"Okay, we'll be waiting," she says as I hear her footsteps retreating back down the stairs.

"Go ahead," I tease Journee.

"No, you go first," she teases back.

"Aww . . . come on."

"I'll go first if you promise not to smack my ass while I leave," she says sternly.

"I can't make any promises. I love your ass. It's so . . ." I don't finish my thought because I get caught up staring right at her ass. That's when Journee rushes out the door.

"Hey, no fair," I yell as I follow after her.

All I can hear is Journee's laughter all the way downstairs. I finally catch up to her at the sliding door leading to the backyard. There is the fire-pit going and a small table. On it sits the graham crackers, chocolate, marshmallows, and some wooden sticks to roast the marshmallows on.

"Wow. You weren't playing," I tell Mom as Journee and I take a seat.

"I told you. I wanted this to be a fun, relaxing weekend." Mom smiles.

Mom proceeds to give Journee and me a wooden stick each, marshmallows at the end. We roast them, twirling the sticks every other minute. Mom and Dad follow suit. We sit, talking about a lot of different topics as we enjoy each other's company.

NINE

Journee

The visit with Knox's parents made me miss my dad. I haven't really kept in touch with him, which is bad on my part. He's the only living parent I have. It's no excuse for me not to keep in touch, but life happened. I've been too busy with my career. Then again, I'm not the only one who could have reached out. Maybe my dad thinks I am not too keen on his new girlfriend, which I wasn't at first. But I came to the realize that my dad just wants to be happy again. Who am I to deny him the right to be happy? Even though he would be with her regardless, it's the principle.

I wasn't necessarily a ball of joy when I heard that he was dating again and basically shutting me out of his life by focusing all his attention on his new girlfriend and her son. Maybe it would have been different if I went with him. Maybe I would have been included in their little family and my dad would acknowledge me more. But I know he was upset, since I decided to stay in North Carolina. Maybe it is time to talk about it.

Knox and the band have a few interviews lined up leading up to the premiere of their new music video. He told me he will be in and out of the apartment for a few days this week. As for me, Phoenix hasn't called or texted me to set up another photoshoot, not since we slept together. I don't know if he feels like he made a mistake by having sex with me. Maybe he thinks he committed the ultimate betrayal, sleeping with his best friend's girl. But it isn't like Knox is all that innocent either. Maybe this is my revenge for all Knox put my through. No, it is. Yet a part of me feels like shit. I don't know why I feel this way. That's why this past weekend, with Knox's parents, I couldn't get myself together. I was overthinking. I tried to act normal in front of Knox, but I just couldn't stop thinking about what happened with Phoenix.

I'll give Phoenix some space. Hopefully, he will contact me in a couple of days. I don't want us having sex together to come between our professional relationship. But I might have fucked that up as well. It took me a while to get to this point in my modeling career, and now I might have to start looking for another studio to work with. I don't want to jump the gun, though. I will wait until Phoenix and I can discuss what happened between us that night.

I have been in my head the whole morning. I need to shake it off. I get up, get dressed, and eat breakfast. Since I have no modeling gigs today, I just spend the day binging reality shows and eating semi-healthy. I settle on the couch and put on the new season of "Seeking Love." I watch two or three episodes, and that's when I notice my life is turning out to be like a reality show. I watch these shows to escape my reality, but now I am feeling sick to my stomach. I quickly switch to watching a movie instead. I am flipping to the channels to look for a movie to watch when my phone vibrated.

Dad: *Hey, baby girl. Pearl and I are in town. I really would love for you to meet her. We are going to this seafood restaurant called The Fisherman's Catch to eat. Can you meet us there at four? You can bring Knox along, if you want.*

Speaking of him, this is the distraction I need. I have wanted to clear the air between us for the longest, even though I don't know if there is anything air to clear. Maybe my mind is playing tricks on me, like with everything else is.

Hey, Dad. I would love to meet you and Pearl. I will be there at four.

The restaurant is twenty minutes away from Knox's apartment. I have never been to this seafood restaurant, but the name sounded interesting— The Fishermen's Catch. I don't really want to meet my dad's girlfriend without something for her. So I stop by the store to pick up some pink carnations. I figure flowers are always a safe bet.

When I arrive at the restaurant, it is semi-packed. The food is likely on point for it to be this packed. That gets me excited. I am a little on the hungry side, so I'm glad my dad wanted me to meet them here.

There is a lady at the host stand. Her name tag reads *Nancy*. "Welcome to the Fisherman's Catch," she says. "How can I help you?"

"I'm looking for my father, Myles Watson," I state.

She looks through the seating chart, before getting up and saying, "Oh, right this way." She leads me to the table where they are sitting at.

"Thank you," I say as she leaves the table.

My dad gets up to give me a hug when he sees me. "Journee, I'm so glad you could come."

"Me too. These are for you, Ms. Pearl," I say, handing her the pink carnations I brought.

"Thank you, sweetie. How thoughtful of you." She smells the flowers before saying, "They're beautiful."

I sit down next to my father. "You're welcome."

"So how's my baby girl doing?" my dad asks eagerly.

"I'm okay. I got signed with a photography studio.

But as soon as the words leave my mouth, I feel the sting of regret. I don't know whether my contract with Phoenix will continue. But I guess I have to wait and see. There is no need to feel guilty until I know what's going through Phoenix's mind.

"Pearl, my daughter is a model," my dad explains. "She's going to be big one day,"

Pearl just smiles and nods. She is a petite woman, around five feet, with curly black hair and brown eyes. She looks the same age as my father. I can kind of see why he'd be drawn to her. Pearl reminds me of my mother to a certain extent. She is a well-kept and put-together woman.

We order our food and continue to talk. Pearl talks about her son and how she met my dad. She and my dad exchange sly looks and smiles as she tells the story. My dad is clearly happy, and that's what my mother would have wanted for him.

"Journee, I asked you here to meet Pearl, but I also

have some news myself to share," he confesses. I look at him, then at Pearl, who has a huge smile on her face. There is no denying what he is going to say.

"We are getting married in the spring," he says excitedly.

"And Myles and I would love for you to be in the wedding," Pearl adds.

"That's wonderful, Dad. I'm happy for you," I state.

"How's Knox's doing?" Dad asks.

"He's doing good. He had interviews this week. One was today, so that's where he's at right now."

"Oh, that's great. When are you two going to get engaged?"

My dad has to hit me with that question. The funny thing is that Knox and I have been dating about as long as Dad and Pearl. This difference is that Knox and I are still young and focused on our careers. My dad and Pearl are older, and they were each married before. I can see how ready they are to settle down.

"Knox and I are too focused on our careers to think about marriage," I explains.

"Seriously? You can get married and still focus on your careers," he states.

"Marriage is a big step, and it changes you whether you want it to or not. I don't think I'm ready for that yet."

"Fair enough. But wouldn't it be easier for you two to settle down? Knox, as a musician and you as a model. You'll be telling the world that you are officially off the market."

I don't want to have this conversation. Knox and I are fine the way we are, and no amount of coercion will make us change our minds. We eventually get off the subject of Knox and I marrying, and back on Dad and Pearl's wedding plans.

"We'll be sending out the wedding invitations soon," Dad states when all the dishes have been taken away.

"We really would like you and Knox to try to make it. That's if you don't have any prior engagements during that time," Pearl adds.

"I will make sure our calendars are clear that weekend," I state.

"Thanks, baby girl. It would mean a lot to us."

I am all set, with my debit card in my hand to pay for my food, when my dad says, "Don't worry about it."

I am like, "Are you sure?" and he nods. My dad doesn't have to pay for my food, but that is the kind of dad he is, and I am grateful for him.

On the drive back to the apartment, I think about the visit with my dad and his fiancée. I'm glad they came to see me and I was able to meet Pearl. I am happy that I got to witness my dad and Pearl's love up close and personal. It was so magical. I look forward to being in their wedding in the spring.

No sooner than I settle back in to relaxation mode my phone vibrates again. Thinking it is Phoenix, I check the message. But it isn't him. It is Chesca.

Chesca: *Hey, Journee. I'm having a girls night tonight and would love for you to come hang with us. That's* *if you have nothing else planned.*

No, nothing planned. I would love to hang with you girls. What time?

Chesca: *Come around eight. And don't worry about bringing anything, I have everything covered. See ya at eight.*

A girls night is just what the doctor ordered. I am not planning on being stressed about Phoenix this weekend. Seeing my dad helped take my mind off it a bit, but a girls night—likely with a lot of alcohol—is certainly going to make me forget. That's exactly what I need.

I text Knox to let him know where I will be before I start getting ready. Hopefully, we will be staying in. I am not about to get all fancy. I throw on some sweats and a hoodie instead.

I put Chesca's address, which she texted, in my GPS. Her condo is about fifteen minutes away. I notice her neighborhood is unusually quiet. It is very well kept. There is no garbage on the ground, and all the condos seem similar on the outside, but I know that there has to be a difference in floor plans.

"Thank you for inviting me to your girls night," I tell Chesca when she opens her front door.

"Hey, girl, no problem. I told you I would," she says. "Come on I'm and have a seat on the couch."

I step inside. "I'm not too underdressed, am I?"

"Girl, no. You see how I'm dressed. We're just staying in." Chesca is wearing pink-and-purple-striped leggings with an oversized solid-pink T-shirt. She doesn't have any makeup on, and her hair is tied up in a messy bun.

"Now come inside. I want you to meet Aspen." She leads me inside and introduces me. "A, I want you to meet Journee. She also models with Phoenix."

Aspen looks like she is about five-nine. She has long blonde hair and light brown eyes. She has black leggings on, and her long flower-print silk top looks kimono inspired.

"Hey, Aspen. Nice to meet you," I say as I take a seat on the couch.

"Same here," Aspen says with a smile.

"Aspen got hired a few months before you," Chesca says from the kitchen. "Journee, are you hungry?"

"Somewhat," I respond.

"I ordered a pizza, half cheese and half pepperoni. It should be here in half an hour. But I thought we would play a little game before it arrived." Chesca comes out of the kitchen holding a few paper plates and a bottle of wine.

"A game?" I question. "What kind of game?"

"It's called Truth Bombs: Sex Edition. I wouldn't say it's a game, per say. But rather us sharing are deep, darkest secrets," Chesca explains, "with no names, of course."

"Okay, I'm scared."

"This should be fun. You won't know who the person is referring to," Aspen says. "So what do you have to be nervous about?"

"Well. Okay, then," I say courageously.

"Who will go first?" Chesca asks, smirking.

"I'll go," Aspen speaks up. "Ummm . . . I once fucked a girl with a boyfriend,"

"You did?" I question.

"They don't called me the "Bi Bitch" for nothing. I don't care who I fuck or who I fuck over,"

"In other words, don't pissed her off," Chesca adds with a laugh.

"Oh, I don't plan to," I reason.

"Okay. My turn," Chesca says. "I fucked a member of a band once."

"Who?" I ask curiously.

"No, no. No names," Aspen says, repeating the rules. "It's your turn, Journee."

I look at both Aspen and Chesca, not knowing if I want to continue with this game. It wouldn't be fair if I don't say who I slept with since they both divulged who they had sex with.

"Okay," I say as I took a deep breath. "I fucked my boss once."

"Ohhh . . . is this a current boss?" Aspen says, trying to pry.

"No names, remember?" Chesca says.

As soon as I give my confession, the doorbell rings.

"Must be the pizza. It's early." Chesca gets up and goes to the door.

I can't help but wonder if the girls know I was talking about Phoenix. I'm glad it was a "no names" type of game.

Chesca comes back and sets the pizza on the coffee table. "Here we are."

We eat in silence, likely thinking about our confessions.

"So wanna watch a movie?" Chesca says, breaking the silence between us.

"Yeah, I would," I state.

"I second that," Aspen responds.

Chesca grabs the TV remote and starts to flip through the channels.

"Wait . . . wait . . . Go back," I say, getting her attention.

Chesca flips back one channel. Aspen recognizes the actress Meg Ryan right away. *You've Got Mail*.

"It's a classic. Let's watch it," I suggest.

TEN

Rush

It's nearly ten am, and I've been texting Aspen all morning. *Where the fuck is she?* We have three months until our wedding, and the wedding planner is coming over to meet with us in half an hour. Granted, we have a few more meetings with our planner, but this is getting down to the wire. The planner suggested from today until the wedding, both the bride and groom be present at all the meetings scheduled.

As I am about to send what seemed like that hundredth text message, Aspen came rushing through the front door. "I'm sorry. I totally forgot that we had to meet with the planner today," Aspen says apologetically.

"Where were you that you couldn't answer my texts?" I ask, annoyed.

"I was at my friend's condo. She was having a girls night."

"Didn't you hear your cell vibrating?"

"I turned it off. I didn't see your texts until I was in the car."

"Oh . . . of course you didn't."

"Let me jump in the shower and freshen up. I'll be quick," Aspen says, rushing into the bathroom.

"She'll be here in half an hour," I remind her.

Sometimes, I don't get Aspen. She knows our wedding is in three months. She supposedly set reminders on her phone to let her know about these meetings. But her phone was off for God knows how long. She obviously didn't get my texts or see the reminders she set.

I quickly straighten up the living room. It is where we usually have these meetings. Then I venture back into the kitchen to grab three bottled waters. Aspen appears as soon as I come back to the living room. She is wearing blue skinny jeans and a nice long blue pin-striped blouse. It has a matching blue belt tied around the waist. And since our meetings are casual, Aspen is wearing fuzzy white slipper socks as well.

"Is she here yet?" she asks.

"No. Not yet. But she should be soon."

Aspen sit quietly on the couch, playing on her phone. The expression on her face is that of a kid on Christmas. *What the hell is she smiling like that for? What is she looking at?* I decide not to question her about it. It is enough that Aspen got a piece of my mind when she came in this morning.

Soon I hear a knock at the door and leave Aspen to whatever she is doing to go get the door. "Hey, Barbara.

Come on in," I say, greeting our wedding planner at the door.

Barbara Sutton works at Sutton's Touch, a family-owned wedding business. They have been in business for five years and had an amazing track record of planning the most spectacular weddings. Aspen is the one who found Barbara. She attended a bridal expo with her bridesmaids a few months after we got engaged. That's where she met Barbara.

Recently, however, I've been the one taking the lead, reminding Aspen of the meetings. Aspen's been too busy with her modeling career to keep up. I don't think that's really an excuse, but if she's going to fall back to focus on her career, I have to step up and take the reins. Most people have heard of bridezillas, but it's kind of fun being the groomzilla for our wedding.

I lead Barbara to our living room. She sits on the couch and pulls her laptop out. "Hi, Aspen," she says.

"Hey, Barbara," Aspen responds, but her attention is still on her phone.

Barbara looks at me with a concern, as if asking if this is a good time to have the meeting. I nod and mouth, "It's okay."

"Aspen, could you put your phone down?" I asked her in the calmest voice I can muster, even though I am fuming inside.

Aspen sets her phone down on the end table next to the couch. Barbara lets out a deep sigh, like she knows we are a failing couple, the kind who don't even make it to their wedding. But I am determined not to let this get to me.

"Okay, let's begin," Barbara finally says.

We go over how we want the venue to be set up, how we want the families to come in, and how we want the wedding processional to come in. Barbara listens to our excitement, frustrations, and concerns about the wedding. By the end of the meeting, Aspen and I feel sure that our wedding will be the talk of the town.

"Do you have any other questions before we wrap things up?" Barbara says as she finishes typing notes on her laptop. Aspen and I didn't

"Well, if there are no more questions. I will be on my way," she closed her laptop and rises from the couch.

"Thank you so much for all you are doing to help us plan our special day," I say.

"No problem. You and Aspen are a very unique couple. And I'm having a blast getting to help you guys."

Aspen has grabbed her phone again, and she looks like she is messaging someone. Barbara looks at me, then Aspen. She smiles and nods at both of us. I don't know what she is thinking, but I don't really want to know. I lead Barbara to the door and thank her again for coming. After she leaves, I go back into the living room to find Aspen not there.

Her phone is face down on the couch. She must have gone to the bathroom. I look at her phone for the longest time, contemplating whether I should go through it or not. I glance down the hall and stare at the closed bathroom door. I am curious. What was Aspen doing on her phone all this time?

I grab her phone and flip it over. *What the hell is this?* There are multiple text messages from a private number. This texts aren't exactly innocent either. One says *I want to watch my girlfriend fuck you while I get off.*

I hear the bathroom door open, and I quickly put her phone back how I found it.

"What are you doing? You look suspicious," Aspen says, eyeing her phone.

I can't hold back my anger. "I went through your phone. What the fuck Aspen?"

"Why are you even going through my phone?" she says, annoyed.

"Who are these texts from?"

"Nobody," she says defensively.

"Oh . . . it's somebody all right." I let out a sinister laugh.

"If you must know, it wasn't consensual," Aspen blurts out. "He forced me to do those things."

"It doesn't sound like that to me," I argue.

"Well, fuck. You're going to believe some stranger over your own fiancée?"

"I don't know who or what to believe, Aspen."

"Then maybe I should give you some space to figure that out."

"Yeah," I mutter.

"I'll stay at my parents." Aspen goes to grab her things

I can't believe it. Aspen and I are three months from our wedding, and she cheats on me.

What the actual fuck, Aspen? Am I not good enough for you?

I watch her leave without saying a word through the front door. Anger rises up within me. Not just at her, but at the asshole who apparently watched Aspen fuck his girlfriend—possibly even fucked her himself.

ELEVEN

Knox

Journee and I spend an hour and a half wiping down kitchen counters, sweeping floors, and vacuuming rugs in preparation for the music video premiere. After, Journee puts out the veggies, crackers, and fruit trays on the tables. I get the soda, beers, and wine out of our refrigerator as well.

"It looks like we're all set," Journee says, looking at our spread. "Now just waiting for everyone to arrive."

I am so excited. I love the fact that everyone always comes to my apartment for the premiere. Getting all of us together never gets old, and I'm very grateful for how long our band has lasted. These get togethers have become something I look forward to every time we shoot a video. It's become a tradition I hope never ends.

"I'm going to freshen up before everyone starts to trickle in," Journee says as she heads to our bedroom.

I decide to call Ezra to see what else he and the others can bring. We have alcohol, but our spread is mostly healthy food. We need some junk food to munch on as well.

"Hey, Knox," Ezra answers cheerfully.

"Hey, I have a little dilemma here," I say.

"What's the dilemma?"

"I need some junk food. All we got is healthy stuff right now."

"I can certainly help you out in that area," Ezra says with a chuckle. "What do you want me to bring? I can call Reid to see if he's willing to bring something too."

"Anything that's not fruit or veggies . . . please."

"I'm on it," Ezra says, imitating a superhero voice.

"Thank you so fucking much. You're a lifesaver."

I survey the living room and what has set up so far. I am pleased with how it turned out. Now I just have to wait for everyone to come. I grab a beer, sit on my couch, and watch TV. Soon Journee joins me with a glass of wine.

"Are you ready for tonight?" she asks curiously.

"So ready! I live for times like this. Much needed bonding time."

"It will be fun see everybody, since I wasn't in the music video. I also can't wait to see the video."

"I can't wait for you to see the music video. It was so fucking fun to make."

I cuddle closer to Journee, and she lays her head on my shoulder as we watch a random show on TV. I lean down to kiss her forehead. Then she brings her lips to mine. I kiss her lips slowly at first before I deepen the kiss. We make out for a good while, until I hear a knock at the door.

Journee pulls away. "They're here. Do you want to get the door, or shall I?"

"Shit . . . I was just . . ." I start to say.. "I'll get it."

Ezra and Reid are the first to arrive. They each have two bags in their hands. I'm assuming it's the junk food I asked them to bring.

"We weren't interrupting anything, were we?" Ezra asks.

Just me trying to fuck my girlfriend before everyone arrives. "No, it's cool. Come on in," I say. "Thanks again for bringing the junk food."

Reid and Ezra enter the apartment, and Reid asks, "Where do you want these?"

"Over here." I show them the table of veggies, fruit, and crackers.

Ezra cocks his head to the side. "You weren't lying."

"We bought some cookies and chips," Reid says, surveying the table.

They unload their bags set everything on the table. Then they grab a seat in the living room.

"Hey, Journee," Ezra says.

"Hey, Ezra. It seems like I haven't seen you guys in forever."

"I know . . . How's modeling been?"

"It's been good. I signed with a photographer."

"Knox told me," Ezra says excitedly. "Congratulations."

I make my way back to the living room too. "Would you like a beer?"

"Yeah," Ezra says.

"One for me too." Reid adds.

I grab two cold beers and hand them to Reid and Ezra. There is another knock at the door. I go to open it, and it is Sarai and Willow.

"Hey, ladies," I say.

"Hey, Knox. Where's Journee?" Sarai asked

"She's in the living room with the boys,"

Sarai and Willow made their way to the living room. The only people I am waiting on are Chesca and Seth. Seth texted me and said he was running a little late but that he'll be here soon. But Chesca, I don't know where she is, or if she plans on coming.

Seth arrives about fifteen minutes later. It is an hour until the music video premiere, so we all chat a bit about different things. Everyone begins to grab more snacks and drinks, waiting in anticipation. As soon as we all settle in front of the TV, there is a knock on the door. I go to go answer the door. It's Chesca.

"Sorry, I'm late," she says apologetically.

"It's okay. The video hasn't started yet. But everyone is here," I say. I lead Chesca into the living room. "Hey, guys, you remember Chesca, right?"

Everyone welcomes her inside. Everyone except Journee, who stares at her like a deer in highlights.

"This is my girlfriend—" I begin.

"Journee?" she says, puzzled.

"Wait. You two know each other?"

"Yeah, we do. She and I model with the same photographer."

By now Journee has a look of both fear and rage on her face. "Connor?" I question.

"No, who's Connor? Phoenix is our photographer," Chesca says.

"Phoenix? As in Phoenix Baldwin?"

"Yup."

By this time, Journee has left the living room and is retreating to our bedroom.

"I'll be back." I leave the group of onlookers in the living room and rush into our bedroom. When I get inside, Journee is pacing the floor with an unrecognizable expression on her face.

"What didn't you tell me you were modeling with Phoenix?" I ask her.

"Because I didn't know how you would feel about it."

"I wouldn't have minded it. But you didn't have to lie about."

Journee continues to pace back and forth in heavy thought. She paces a few times more, stops in her tracks, and shoots dagger eyes at me. "You fucked her, didn't you?" she says angrily.

"What?"

"You heard me . . . You fucked her."

I start to sweat as I try to figure out how the hell she would have known. "Umm . . ."

"You're an asshole." Journee spits the words out as she says them.

I hang my head in defeat. She is right. I have been the biggest asshole to her all these years. I don't know what I did to have deserved her. But I keep fucking up, and I knew it would eventually blow up in my face. Tonight is that night. I try to embrace her. Journee slaps me across my face.

"Fuck you," she yells.

It takes me a minute to regain my composure. This is certainly not how I want this night to go. Journee locks herself in our bathroom. I let her be and go back out into the living room.

"Is everything okay?" Seth says, concerned.

"I'm sorry, but I think everyone should leave right now," I announce. "It's not a good time."

Everyone looks at one another and starts to pack up their things. Soon everyone is gone. Everyone but Chesca. She is still standing there, waiting for me to explain myself, I guess. But there is nothing to explain to her. Only that I'm a complete and utter fuck-up.

"Your girlfriend isn't that innocent either," Chesca says with her arms folded against her chest.

"What? What do you mean?"

"Oh, she didn't tell you. Of course she wouldn't have." She glares at me intensely, not breaking our eye contact.

"Tell me what?"

"She fucked Phoenix." Chesca smirks at her own words.

"You're lying. You're a fucking liar."

"Just like you omitted the fact you had a girlfriend, right?"

I just look at her and shake my head. This has been one of the worst nights of my life, and it couldn't get any worse. Then Journee comes out of our room, carrying her duffel bag. She looks between Chesca and me with disgust. She starts walking to the door, and I grab her arm.

"Get the fuck off me," she yells.

"Journee, please don't go. Let me explain," I plead.

"And why is she still here? Were you planning to fuck her while I was in our bedroom?"

"Journee, please . . ."

I look into her eyes only to see hurt, pain, and betrayal in them. I notice that she had been crying, because her eyes were red and puffy.

"Why don't ask her?" Chesca cuts in. "I'm sure you want to know the truth."

I completely forgot about her. She needs to leave— and fast. I need this moment to be between Journee and me.

"I think you need to leave. Now," I say urgently.

"All right, I'll go." She heads to the door. She opens it but stops and glances back at Journee. "Girl, you need to leave him and never look back."

After she leaves, I notice I am still holding Journee's arm. Journee snatches it away and heads toward the door too.

"Before you leave, tell me this. Is it true?" I question.

Journee stands there for a second. I can tell her heart is breaking. She doesn't know what to feel or how to feel about me. Journee is contemplating whether or not to confess the truth.

"Yes, it's true," she finally states. Then she leaves.

I am in complete and utter shock. Journee slept with Phoenix, my best friend of all guys. I go into the kitchen and grab two beers. I want to numb this pain. I don't want to feel anything. So I sit on the couch and look around at my empty apartment and drink my beers. This was supposed to have been a night to remember, but it turned out to be a night from hell. I am not sure how long I sat and wallowed when the doorbell rung once more. I rush to the door thinking it is Journee, but when I open the door, I am met with a guy who doesn't look so happy to see me.

"Hello, can I help you?" I say, a bit disappointed it isn't who I want to see.

"Do you know a girl named Aspen?" he questions.

"Who?"

"She's my fiance, and she says you forced her to fuck your girlfriend. Is this true?"

I thought long and hard about who this Aspen girl is. I don't . . . oh fuck . . . now I remember—long blonde hair and light brown eyes. I met her at a concert and was immediately attracted to her because she was bold and unapologetic. I didn't even notice if she had a ring or not. I guess that's why her fiancé is here now trying to find answers.

"Who are you, and how did you find me?"

"That's not the point," he says angrily. "Did you or didn't you have your girlfriend fuck my fiancee'?"

"Hell no. Your fiancée is lying. You better leave before I call the police," I tell him.

I am getting scared. I don't know this guy from Adam, and he just shows up on my doorstep, demanding answers, asking whether or not I forced Journee to fuck his fiancée. On top of that, he won't tell me how he found me or who he is.

"No need to call them. They'll surely come." He smirks and pulls out a gun.

The first shot hits me in my chest. I fall to the ground, gripping the area around my heart. I hear him laughing. He continues firing rounds as bullets penetrate my body.

TWELVE

Journee

I get in my car and drive. I don't know where I am going, but I know I need to clear my head. Tonight isn't the best of nights. I don't know how in the hell it turned out this way. *How could Chesca betray me like this?* She had to know who Knox was and that he was taken. Maybe she didn't care. I knew something was a little suspicious that night at her condo. She had said she slept with someone in a band, but I didn't put two and two together until she showed up at our apartment. That's when it clicks, that dumb bitch. She's also a bitch for ratting me out to Knox about sleeping with Phoenix.

I end up at Phoenix's condo. Even though we haven't talked since the night we slept together, I have to know. I have to know how Phoenix felt about that night. He be shocked I'm here, no doubt, but I need closure. I got closure with Knox; I need closure with Phoenix. That night I slept with Phoenix, I felt at home. It was a different feeling than I had with Knox. I wonder if Phoenix sensed that. He was kind of taken aback when I said I wished he had stolen me from Knox. I wonder if that made him feel guilty.

When I arrive at his condo, I wait in my car for a few minutes to collect my thoughts and figure out what I am going to say to him.

Phoenix answers the door quickly when I knock. Black-and-white pajama bottoms, a black shirt, and a mess for hair—he looks like he'd been woken up from a deep sleep, but his eyes seem to light up once he sees me standing there.

"Journee, what are you doing here?"

"Can I come in? It's been one hell of a night," I tell him.

I follow Phoenix inside and sit on his couch. I can't help but think about the last time I was here, how he pleasured me on this couch and how I wouldn't mind him doing it again.

"Do you want something to drink?" Phoenix says, shaking me out of my thoughts.

"Water, please."

When Phoenix comes back with a bottle of water. He hands it to me and sits next to me on the couch. "So what happened?"

"I found out Knox slept with Chesca," I state.

"And how did you find this out?"

"We played a game when I went to her apartment for a girls night she invited me to. During the game, Chesca said that she had fucked a band member once."

"Oh shit."

"So when she came to Knox's apartment to watch the music video, I realized it was him she was talking about," I explain.

"Oh . . . so what happened after you found out?"

"I left and came here. I didn't know where else to go," I say honestly.

"Are you two broken up?"

I hesitate for a second. "I guess we are."

"So what does that mean for us?"

"Umm . . . I really don't know. I wasn't sure if you wanted anything to do with me after we slept together. You didn't contact me afterward, so I figured you didn't care."

"That is so far from the truth. I cared then, and I care now. I told you I always had a thing for you. But I didn't want to step on Knox's toes," he says. "But now that you've broken up with him, maybe I have a chance?"

"When we slept together, I felt like I was home in yours arms. I never felt that way with Knox," I explain. "He was always so hot and cold. Demanding and demeaning."

"So what are you saying, Journee?"

"I'm saying I want to give this a try." Phoenix pulls me into an embrace and kisses me lightly on this lips. "I could get used to this," I whisper to him.

Phoenix looks intensely in my eyes. "Me too."

I am not worried about getting the rest of my stuff from Knox's apartment. I can do that tomorrow . . . or anytime really. I'm pretty sure Knox knows that we are done. So I'm okay with being with Phoenix tonight.

We decide to watch TV, and Phoenix starts to flip through channels. There isn't anything good on, so he just turns to a random news channel. At first they are talking about the weather for tomorrow: sunny with no chance of rain.

"We could do an outdoor photoshoot, if you're up for it," Phoenix suggests.

"That's would be fun," I say.

We continue to talk about the possibility, and then the news anchor interrupts with breaking news:

I'm here at Cove Gardens apartments, where a shooting took place this evening. The victim was twenty-six-year-old guitarist Knox Foster of the rock band Supposed Posers. There were no other casualties, and the shooter has been taken into custody . . .

I can't believe what I am hearing. I just left Knox's apartment. I started to shake uncontrollably. What the fuck? I turn to Phoenix, and he pulls me into his arms. I begin bawling. He holds me and lets me cry into his shirt, pulling me close and slightly rocking me to calm me down.

I pull away from him after a while and stare into space. This is a bad dream. This isn't real. I can't accept this. I can't accept Knox is gone. I remember slapping him across the face and telling him to fuck off. I feel the sting of that, the weight of the words I said.

At that moment, I wish I could take all of that back. I feel like shit. Yes, Knox cheated on me and did some fuck up things to me through the years. But that was his last memory of me— us fighting. What a horrible way to die;

knowing you and your ex-girlfriend just had a fight.

"Journee . . ." Phoenix whispers. I turn my head toward him, tears staining my cheeks.
"This is just as much a shock to me as it is to you. I fucking can't believe this shit," he says angrily.

"This is too much to handle right now," I confess.

"This *is* too much. It hit too close to home," he says.

"Phoenix, I . . . I think it might be a good idea to move in with my dad," I explained   "But you didn't want to live with him before. Do you think he would want you to live with him now?"

"I'm not sure. The only way to find out it to ask him."

"But for how long would you be with him?" Phoenix says.

"At least until after my father's wedding."

"Oh . . ."

"I know you are worried about us. But you have nothing to worry about," I assure him. "I will be back. I just need some time away."

"I understand. This was so unexpected."

"No shit. This was a wake-up call for all of us," I say honestly.

"Are you going to call your dad to explain the situation?"

"I should, shouldn't I?"

"Yes, you should. Would you like me to give you

some privacy while you talk with him?" Phoenix asks.

"No, I want you here."

I need him here because I know the call is going to be one of the hardest calls of my life. I need Phoenix's support in case he needs to speak for me in case I am too distraught that I can't continue to talk.

"I'm here," he says, squeezing my hand. "I'm not going anywhere."

I make the call, and Phoenix sits next to me and starts to rub my back as I wait for my dad to answer.

"Hey, baby girl," my dad says. "Missing us already?"

"Yes . . ." My voice cracks.

"Journee, what's wrong?"

I start to tear up. "Dad, Knox was killed tonight."

"What!!! Are you hurt?"

"No, I'm okay. It's my heart that hurts."

"Do you want us to come back to pick you up?" he asks.

"Uh-huh. I . . . I want to come live with you."

"Thank goodness," he says, relieved. "I can't have you this far away and be worrying about you. Especially now since this happened."

I look at Phoenix, and he kisses my forehead. "Babe, we'll get through this. Don't worry too much."

"I know," I whisper back.

"Dad, I'm going to go now and start packing," I say into the phone.

"Alright, I'll be getting on the road to come get you soon."

EPILOGUE

Six Months Later

" A re you ready to head back?" my dad asks.

"Yes," I say, packing my things. "Thank you for allowing me to stay for this long. I really needed the time away."

"You're welcome, baby girl. Anytime," he raves. "Have you spoken to Phoenix, letting him know you're heading back there soon?"

"I did. I made sure to let him know when I would be arriving." I reassure him.

In the span of six months of living with my dad and his new wife, I've learned a lot about the journey I'm on. I watched my dad and step-mom get married in a beautiful spring wedding. I finally met my step-brother, Sawyer, who already had a very beautiful girlfriend, who was his date. The whole ceremony was special, and they honored both my mom and Sawyer's dad by integrating a piece of them into the wedding. During the reception, both of our parents had a surprise for us and invited us on their honeymoon with them. At first I thought it would be awkward, but they explained that Sawyer and I would have separate rooms and the freedom to explore the island without them. So it turned out well. It was like we were on our own little vacation.

When my dad and I are talking, Pearl stops by my room. She is wearing a black terry cloth robe with black-and-white polka dot slippers. Her hair is protected underneath a black bonnet. Even after just waking up, Pearl has a calm and peaceful demeanor that radiates around her. It is very infectious and saturated the entire room.

"I wanted to say, it was great to have you here. It was really a pleasure getting to know you," she explains.

"I had a great time as well," I state. "I'm glad my dad met you. I can see you make him so happy."

"Can I give you a hug?" Pearl asks politely.

"Oh. Of course."

Pearl gives me the biggest hug imaginable. I want to stay in her embrace. It is so warm and full of love. Just like the hugs my mom used to give. After our embrace, my dad whispers something to her, kisses her, and then she goes on her way.

"You have to come back again, sweetie. And next time, you'll have to bring Phoenix with you," he suggests.

"I will definitely bring Phoenix with me," I state.

"Well, finish packing. We'll get on the road in a few."

I give him a hug before I continue packing my belongings.

I quickly grab breakfast on the go and say my good-byes to Pearl and Sawyer, who are now dressed and eating breakfast at the kitchen table. I am definitely going to be back sooner rather than later. I've grown to love my new family. I am not sure at first, but after staying with them this long, my love for them has grown exponentially.

My dad grabs my suitcase as we both walk out to his car. He puts my suitcase in the trunk and slams the trunk closed. Before we leave, we both look to the open front door. Both Sawyer and Pearl are waving at us. We wave back, and then we are off.

The whole drive back takes over three hours, and we have to stop to grab lunch at some point. Once we get to Phoenix's condo, I ask my dad if he wants to come in for a bit, but he needs to get back. So I reach over to give him a hug, and he kisses me on my cheek.

"I'm going to miss you, baby girl," my dad says. "Take care of yourself."

"I'm going to miss you too," I state. "And don't worry. I will."

I embrace him one more time before he leaves. I knock on Phoenix's door and stand back. The door flings open, and there stood Phoenix in gray sweats and a black hoodie on. His blond was hair all disheveled, his eyes shining brighter than the stars in the night sky.

He embraces me and gives me an earth-shattering kiss. "Babe, I missed you so much."

"I missed you too," I tell him.

"Where's your dad?" Phoenix questions.

"He had to get back. But I told him you'd be coming with me next time I visited them."

"Oh, I would love that." He grabs my suitcase and says with a laugh, "Now get in here."

We settle on the couch and stare at each other for the longest time, like we are in awe that we're back together again.

"So what have you been doing while I was away," I ask Phoenix.

"I've been working and hanging out with Reid and Ezra."

"Oh." I grow concerned. "How are they doing?"

"They are doing wonderfully. They recently had a joint marriage ceremony, actually. They said life was too short, so they didn't want to wait to get married. The ceremony was beautiful but short and to the point."

"Oh, wow. Congrats to them." I grin. But then my grin turns somber. "How are they dealing with Knox's death? I know it's been six months, but still."

"They are handling it okay. They decided to stop playing shows, but they got matching tattoos on their wrists to remember Knox by. It's a guitar pick with the letter *K* on the inside," he says.

"Oh, that's a shame, but it's sweet that they could do something to honor his memory."

"You're okay with that?"

"Yeah, I am. He was still part of the band. What he did to me was my thorn to bear, not theirs," I explain. "And Knox's killer? How did he find Knox?"

"I heard on the news that Rush Cantor was secretly following the band to keep tabs on him. They said that he was Knox's childhood bully," he explains.

"I never knew Knox was bullied growing up," I respond. "So what happen to Rush? Did he get jail time?"

"Only two years." Phoenix shakes his head in disbelief "The police said he was only defending his fiancée, who claimed that Knox raped her. But the judge overturned their statement and sentenced Rush to two years because it was technically assault.

"What! That's some bullshit! Two fucking years? That's it?" I say, shocked.

"At least he got that. He could have gotten off," Phoenix explains.

"But he killed a man, and do we really know if the fiancée was telling the truth?"

"I guess we'll never really know the actual truth."

"Our judicial system is a joke. That's a slap on the fucking wrist. But at least Reid and Ezra have their wives now and can finally move on with their lives," I say.

"Tell me about it. But yeah, I'm glad Ezra and Reid can finally move on with their lives. I wish nothing but the best for them."

Phoenix and I talk for a little bit longer about what we want our lives to look like. We all learned and grew from this tragedy. I realized my home would always be with Phoenix. I can't imagine my life without him in it.

ACKNOWLEDGEMENTS

Kimberly See:
Your comments and suggestions during the editing process of "Illicit Dose Of Chaos," helped a great deal to make my book better than it originally was. So thank you.

Diana TC:
Thank you so much for making me another EPIC cover design for "Illicit Dose Of Chaos."

Jo McCall (Wicked Gypsy Designs)
Thank you so much for the amazing chapter designs that you did for "Illicit Dose Of Chaos."

Mackenzie (NiceGirlNaughtyEdits):
Thank you so much for making the teasers for "Illicit Dose Of Chaos." I loved them so much!

Family and Friends:
Thank you so much for the continued support of me and my books. I love you all.

Regina Ann Faith is a Lyricist, Poet, Writer, Composer and Author. She graduated with a B.A in Communications/Film. This is her first rockstar romance series titled The Love Sick Series. The second book in this series titled Illicit Dose Of Chaos is the conclusion of Journee and Knox's toxic love story. She can be found on her social media pages at:

www.facebook.com/AuthorReginaAnnFaith

www.twitter.com/ReginaAnnFaith

www.instagram.com/ReginaAnnFaith

www.soundcloud.com/ReginaAnnFaith